ONE DAY A

A Thought for

A Prayer For Each Morning

Please help me walk a Godly way,
With tolerance throughout this day,
It is not for tomorrow that I pray,
But a guiding light to shine today.

Please help me see the Spirit sign,
And understand the truth sublime
Of the sanctity of being kind,
As I live my life one day at a time.

Presented by Betty and Ken Collins

Regency Press (London & New York) Ltd.
125 High Holborn, London WC1V 6QA

ISBN 0 7212 09009

Printed and bound in Great Britain by
Buckland Press Ltd., Dover, Kent.

This book is dedicated to –

TWO WONDERFUL PEOPLE

No matter what the chance in life,
If things went wrong or turned out right,
She always gave a helping hand,
Was ever there to understand,
She guided kindly, made her point,
Gave sympathy of the right amount,
She smiled her way through toil and doubt,
And knew what courage was about,
Always ready for some fun,
With a cheery word for everyone.
This was her policy of life –
A kindly daughter and loving wife,
Promoted now with those who love her,
This lovely lady is my mother.

And yet another fills my mind,
A quiet gentleman, and kind,
Strong in purpose and intent,
Yet gently through his life he went,
Each kindly thought and action given
Sincerely, with the mark of heaven.
Calm courage in adversity,
Believing people should be free
To choose the pathway that they tread,
And answer for the life they've led.
A tower of strength if things went wrong,
A baritone in thought and song,
Who earned his place in God's hereafter,
This generous gentleman is my father.

FOREWORD

One Day at a Time is a quiet calendar of thoughts – an attempt to point a more satisfactory way of thinking and therefore living – a more contented and fulfilling way of life.

The wonders and advantages of modern technology often disguise the disadvantages and basic simplicity of life on earth, until technology could become the master instead of the servant it is intended to be. Technology can work apparent miracles, as mankind is allowed to discover its endless potentials, but in the wrong hands, steered by wrong minds, it can bring suffering to individual scales of life or wreak complete havoc of undreamt of proportions. The choice is ours – "Whether 'tis nobler in the mind to suffer the slings and arrows of outrageous fortune, or take arms against a sea of troubles, and by opposing – end them," always bearing in mind that Mankind has himself created that 'sea of troubles.'

It is not too late to plug the hole that has allowed many decent moral values to drain away almost unnoticed. It is neither too difficult nor too late to reappraise the true uncomplicated values that are the rock foundation on which real happiness is built. It is simply a matter of reorganizing our thinking, becoming aware of the shining goal ahead, and each one of us having the courage to move in that direction. By our example, others will know us, and some will follow.

All the basic knowledge is there already, we only need to recognise it, bring it once more to the surface of life – and use it. By discarding greed and selfishness, and relearning the values of kindness and sharing, we step some way towards the bright star of happiness. By rediscovering the natural miracles of our world, we can become much closer to the power that most of us call God.

Just a thought a day in that direction, can lay the foundation for a peace of mind few of us would think possible. A smile, a hand outstretched, a kindly thought – all we need to start the world on the road to recovery – a pathway of happiness for all, leaving behind the cruelty and pain that is currently being inflicted on other life on earth, we can recreate the balance of life that has been pushed out of shape by mankind so carelessly for so long. One thought at a time, one day at a time towards the shining star of true happiness.

INTRODUCTION

This book is a mixture of the profound and the funny. Presented as a thought for each day of the year, it seeks to help, amuse or inform – as the case may be at the time. An assortment of rhyme, rhythm and prose, the offering for each day settles into its own place – perhaps as a giggle or a smile, maybe with some thought provoking facts or possible dreams – each one with food for thought, for even the giggles – although intended to brighten a day – also present useful ideas for an enquiring mind to gather.

I have enjoyed receiving these pieces and collating them into a breakfast 'serial' that I hope our readers will also enjoy, for the fibre is there in full measure, plus the milk and honey to blend it into very digestible food for the soul.

I wish you happy reading each day – all through the year.

Sincerely,

Betty Collins.

JANUARY

THE SNOWDROPS OF LIFE

JANUARY 1ST

A new opportunity

A NEW YEAR'S DAY

Can point the way, to start a special fashion,
Through a gracious mind of a higher kind,
To lend the world compassion.

JANUARY 2ND

A personal choice

TWENTY-FOUR HOURS

Time – the precious gift that is given to each one of us in equal measure for each day of our lives, and it is for each individual to choose the way they use their own gift of this time. Some will use it for personal material gain, whilst others will use the opportunity to help others less fortunate than themselves. Many will be too lazy to use it at all, but a few with disabilities that make tasks difficult, will nevertheless find a way of using this precious gift wisely and well.

Many people will grumble their way through their twenty-four hours, or use a sharp tongue to prick or wound a fellow human being, or bring suffering to an animal with ruthless action. A few will use their time dishonestly, probably at the expense of someone else. But other folk will recognise their blessings and offer kindly words and actions wherever they are needed, with perhaps, a smile and silent thanks for the gift of time that day.

13

MEMORIES AND FUTURE PATHWAYS

There are three main phases to all life – the past, the present and the future. Of these, the present is the most fleeting.

Its importance lies in the fact that your present thought and action immediately becomes the past. It cannot in itself be altered or eradicated, it has occurred in a moment of the present, to become a station of the past that can only affect the future.

We scarcely realise how brief the present is, until we reflect that each word I write here, is in the present, yet immediately I pass on to the next word, the previous one becomes the past, the one to follow will be in the future. Thus our whole lives are made up of these tiny moments of the present that rush towards us without pause, stay but a moment and then travel on to the past and into our memories.

JANUARY 4TH
Careful gardeners

SEEDS OF LIFE

Most of us know
     That we reap as we sow,
So it's folly to live life unkindly,
     For seed that's unkind
Will most certainly find
     The soil, for to grow quite unsightly.

It's better to sow
     Some seed that will grow
Into beauty, compassion and love,
     For these plants will give pleasure
And live on for ever,
     With guidance from heaven above!

14

CAT CHAT

Said the Persian to the Alley Cat,
"Why are you digging there?
Our gardener has just planted seeds
Of flowers fine and rare."

The Alley Cat went digging on,
His purpose to fulfil,
And then he thought he'd stop and talk,
This Persian Queen to thrill.

Said he "My owner's old and poor,
So can't plant flower seeds,
It's vegetables that she must grow
To satisfy her needs.

So have a thought my Persian Queen,
Put on your thinking cap,
When I have digging I must do,
I'll not spoil her veggie patch."

There are many thoughts to think
On the way things should be done,
Some from folk of high esteem,
Some from humbler sources come.

HIDE AND SEEK

Happiness is like the child's game of Hide and Seek. Many people hide away from themselves, and often other people – and everyone tries to find this elusive happiness. A few realize that happiness is discovered when you actually give it to someone else!

JANUARY 7TH
Wise thinking

LEARNING

Some people learn much faster than others, but this is only to their advantage if they acquire the right knowledge and then learn to use it in the right way, with kindness and compassion and by sharing with others, otherwise their knowledge and the time used in learning has been wasted, and may even do great harm.

JANUARY 8TH
A brighter future?

A LOVING WORLD

If the whole world stopped loving,
  As some people often do,
The world would be a sorry place
  For the likes of me and you.

But if all the world were kinder,
  With dreams of peace at last,
Then all the world could say goodbye
  To the shadows of the past.

JANUARY 9TH
First things first

FROM SEED TO FLOWER

How can anything good ever be done if no-one ever thought of it in the first place? How can the thought blossom into action unless it is fed and watered by a human hand?

FOR TOMORROW'S CHILDREN

People, as inhabitants of this planet, have greater power over its destiny than any other earthly living thing. Only the sea and the land itself have greater power on earth, and we abuse them at our peril.

The earth can split in earthquakes, or breathe fire and destruction with volcanic eruption. The seas can wash away mountains and coastlines, and overwhelm mankind's puny efforts to control it. Only God, manifesting as nature has the greater power of control. The power of mankind is shown to be insignificant by comparison with these, but he has the opportunities and knowledge to work in unison with nature, and use its natural power for right and wise reasons – for compassionate effects instead of the destruction and pain.

By working with nature instead of constantly challenging her, we can still make our world a wonderful place in which to live. For the sake of the children of today and many years hence, we must change our thinking now. How else can we offer happiness to tomorrow's children?

★ ★ ★

JANUARY 11TH
Some day

TOWARDS THE END OF SHAME

Some day, Mankind will hear
The cry of slaughtering pain,
And know we need not cause such fear,
And the call won't be in vain.
When animals no longer die
To feed the vanity of man,
The human race, with head held high
Will end the slaughterers' shame.

17

JANUARY 12TH
A positive thought

GENTLE PERSUASION

More can be accomplished by gentle persuasion than by the use of force. Gentle persuasion seeks to improve and create the worthwhile, force always seeks to destroy. The former is positive, the latter negative because it merely promotes more force in self defence. Only gentle persuasion creates good results through co-operation and agreement.

★ ★ ★

JANUARY 13TH
Life in tune

HAPPINESS

Happiness is not money,
   Worldly goods or fashion's clothes,
Unless they are shared with other folk –
   As the wise soul truly knows.

It's not status or position
   Unless they earn affection,
Teamed with trust and true respect,
   And touched by kindly action.

For happiness is knowing
   How to do the best we can,
To live and love with hearts in tune
   With God's own master plan.

★ ★ ★

JANUARY 14TH
Words in tune

POETRY OF LIFE

WORDS can be the poetry of life, or the harsh sound of an orchestra out of tune with itself – it depends on the way they are used, and their purpose.

JANUARY 15TH
A combined effort

PEOPLE POWER

When enough people are thinking along the same lines for the right reasons, and enough of them have the courage of their convictions, they can work apparent miracles.

★ ★ ★

JANUARY 16TH
A good example

KIND HEARTS

So many people in this world
Use kindly thought and action
To improve the lot of another soul,
And ease away their tension.

With all the bad things that we hear,
It's easy to forget,
The extent of generous kindly hearts,
And the example that they set.

★ ★ ★

JANUARY 17TH
So many uses

SILENCE IS GOLDEN No. 1

. . . It should be and certainly can be, but like everything else that is worthwhile, it can be used well or badly. It can create perfection for one person while some may use it to sulk or show disapproval. Others may use it to hide a truth they don't wish others to know, or in cowardly fashion remain silent when to speak would help or even save another's life. May those who misuse the gift of silence learn its true value, and become aware of the inner knowledge and peace of mind that it brings, and realise at last that Silence is Golden.

On second thoughts

BIG HEADS?

I wonder why Mankind assumes so easily, that he is superior in every respect of life on earth? Many examples of the animal kingdom can be found that should put our own ideas on the subject to shame.

The patience of a pet dog or cat with its owner is an example almost anyone can observe for themselves. The loyalty and sometimes bravery of dogs and horses towards their owners is almost legendary.

A Court Judge may refer to a rapist as behaving like an animal, overlooking the fact that animals do not indulge in rape. Their sexual activity is confined to the specific times when it is designed for the continuation of the species. People are more promiscuous.

Most birds and animals care for and guard their offspring with a dedication that should stir the conscience of some human parents. Neither do most animals indulge in cruelty for the sake of it, this is a particularly unpleasant trait of many humans, who not only deliberately inflict cruelty, but actually enjoy it, unless of course they are on the receiving end!

It seems we should learn a thing or two about the animal kingdom before our heads get too big for our hats!

★ ★ ★

JANUARY 19TH
Its free!

SMILE TIME

A smile will cost us nothing,
    And uses up so little time,
One smile can brighten someone's day –
    Just like this funny rhyme!
So surely we could smile more,
    To make the world look fine,
It's free for all to give and take,
    Yet it never was a crime!
So come on – let's have one big grin
    And make our dull lives shine!

JANUARY 20TH
Jolly good healing

LAUGHTER

Sometimes laughter has a healing quality that puts it in a place apart, to shine as a gem of life as long as memory prevails.

JANUARY 21ST
Brief encounters

FLEETING MOMENTS

Every moment of each day
    Is a priceless gift of time,
To do the very best we may,
    The hills of life to climb.

And as each moment passes by,
    Never to return,
It's up to us to smile or cry,
    And show some real concern.

And as those moments fly away,
    Becoming history,
Let's not forget they make each day
    Of truth and mystery.

JANUARY 22ND
Giggle time

OW!!

What's that sitting on my head?
    I think it's a pain in the neck,
I wonder what its doing there?
    It don't 'arf tickle by heck!

21

JANUARY 23RD
Simplicity

THE SNOWDROPS OF LIFE

The simplest things in life can so often give us the greatest pleasure. They often have a value beyond the most expensive possession. The unexpected smile or helping hand in time of trouble, the first snowdrop on a cold winter's day – trembling nervously in the pale January sunshine. On such moments our happiness can so easily depend.

★ ★ ★

JANUARY 24TH
A way of life

LIFE IN HARMONY

A life that's lived in love and harmony
Will add its portion of world peace eventually.
A love that's given calmly and unselfishly,
Will shine upon the world with spirituality.
And those who know this sacrifice and mystery,
Will also know the blessings of God's sanctity.

★ ★ ★

JANUARY 25TH
Blending souls

TRUE FRIENDS

A true friend is the one who accepts us as we are, tolerates our imperfections, guides us with diplomacy, sighs with us in our own sorrows, smiles with us and at us – at the right moments, and laughs at the same jokes as we do. A true friend knows the meaning of loyalty, and knows they can share their troubles with us. They often think the same thoughts as us at the same time, they know the way to trust and be trusted, and share kindly laughter with us for all the right reasons. They are true friends indeed.

22

JANUARY 26TH
Hidden Beauty

THE SEEING EYE

This world of ours is not the dreadful place some people would have us believe. It is a place of great beauty for those who have the eyes to see. Only the darker thoughts and actions of mankind spoil the view.

JANUARY 27TH
Hidden opportunities

PERCHANCE TO CARE

If life were very easy,
And no-one needed any help,
How could we show compassion
Or sacrifice the self?

If sorrow was not part of life,
How could we know relief,
Or greet a friend with a helping hand
When their road is long and steep?

The mix of fun and sadness
Can sometimes seem unfair,
But it must be right and helpful
When it shows us how to care.

The pattern of each life is planned,
The paths are well defined
To use the opportunities
To care, and just be kind.

JANUARY 28TH
Inner wisdom

TOLERANCE – a wisdom of the soul.

JANUARY 29TH
Knowledge in disguise

ANTS

Have you ever noticed
The perseverance of the ants?
The way they organise themselves
With nothing left to chance?

In the face of all adversity,
No matter what the call,
It's all of them for each of them,
And each one of them for all.

Mankind with his superior schemes
For ruling all the world,
Has still not found a master plan
For the ants to be controlled.

Boiling water, pesticides,
A well aimed heel or fire,
Are still the basic weapons
For his compatriots to admire.

Yet through all this adversity
And catastrophic ant events,
United action and true loyalty
Are still their main defence.

Perhaps mankind is not so wise
Or clever as he thought,
Maybe the loyal teamwork
Is the lesson ants have taught!

This thought should prompt the logic,
That no-one is so wise,
That better lessons can't be learnt
From knowledge in disguise.

JANUARY 30TH
Another way

It is A WISE SOUL that learns by the experiences of others.

The mixture – to be taken daily

MORNING BLESSINGS

The blessings of the morning
  Come to start each day anew,
But we often overlook them,
  Prayerful thanks are far too few.

The sun may rise with dawning,
  To greet our brand new day,
To help our food and flowers to grow,
  And teach us how to pray.

The sky may gleam with azure blue,
  To heal an aching heart,
Or shine with sunrise glowing pink
  To light our daily path.

Sometimes clouds will start our day,
  Bring rest from glaring sun,
The soft grey light of morning,
  With quiet thoughts for everyone.

The rain may drift with gentle flow
  Across our fields and gardens,
Refreshing every leaf and flower,
  A symbol of God's pardon.

Our driving rain will wash away
  The debris we create,
Keep our rivers flowing free –
  Refill a drying lake.

A gentle breeze may softly touch
  A flower in full bloom,
To waft the precious gift they have
  Of nature's sweet perfume.

Perhaps the biting winds of change
  That howl through chimney pots,
Will also prune a rotting branch
  From our precious tall tree tops.

For all life needs God's shaping,
   To keep it pure and true,
And He often uses nature's tools
   To show what we should do.

Thus the morning blessings teach us,
   Supplying all our needs,
We only need to recognise
   The mercy of God's deeds.

FEBRUARY

TIT FOR TAT

FEBRUARY 1ST
Cool magic

FEBRUARY

Icicles hang glowing pink,
  Reflecting from the morning sun,
February's icy link
  Hiding all the joys to come,
– After winter's frost.

FEBRUARY 2ND
A magic glow

HEARTS OF GOLD

Hearts of gold appear in many guises and often in unexpected places. I watched a real Cor Blimey Cockney rummaging beneath his street market stall, to produce a packet of sandwiches, not to satisfy his own hunger, but to feed a rather tatty looking London sparrow that appeared to have a broken leg. His gentle caring attitude as he fed this injured little bird, indicated a real heart of gold beneath a rough exterior, while his customers awaited their turn for attention.

Every now and then, an observant eye can watch an act of generosity with time, money or possession from someone who can ill afford to spare any of these. Someone somewhere will open the door of heart or home to help a fellow human being – or maybe an animal – that is in need of those particular gifts. Such unsung heroes and heroines are everywhere, though often unnoticed – a pure generosity.

In times of bad news, greed and violence, it is easy to feel that the outlook is stormy and even hopeless, and it is well worth noting the many hearts of gold that wander quietly through life uplifting the sad and lonely, and creating the bright light of compassion to illuminate a better pathway for humanity to follow. It seems to be the chosen task of life for some people, and for the rest – gratitude for the example they set, with a chance to emulate them. These hearts of gold are not always easy to find, because they may not belong to people of position or power, they may not be in public eye through television or spectacular news items. The search however, is well worth while, they may be just next door, in a bus queue or supermarket store, the local Post Office or nearby farmyard. Hearts of gold can be found anywhere, and shine with a magic glow that defies their humble origin and value.

FEBRUARY 3RD

Today's little nonsense rhyme reminds us of four pieces of sound advice:–
1. The futility of envy. 2. The value of recognising the difference between our wants and our needs. 3. The necessity of counting our blessings. 4. Above all, the fact that worthwhile lessons of life can be learnt from laughter, or even just a smile.

GOOD NEWS SHOES

The centipede walked happily
  On all his hundred legs,
Until he met a millipede
  Who had a million legs instead.

"Why have you got more legs than me?
  It really isn't fair,
They're very useful things are legs,
  When you wear them by the pair."

The millipede just raised a smile,
  "You are a silly billy,
I have to buy a million shoes
  And wear them willy nilly!"

"Now you my friend can cut the cost
  Of the things you think you want,
One hundred shoes are all you need
  To take your daily jaunt."

"Remember, envy is no help
  To see you through each day,
Life's all swings and roundabouts,
  It seems it's made that way."

So the centipede just toddled on
  In his fifty pairs of shoes,
Counting all those blessings,
  For they really were good news!

FEBRUARY 4TH
The human touch

GOOD INTENTIONS are thoughts from the soul – that need human action to bring them to fruition.

Magic circles

THE CIRCLE OF LIFE

All life on earth is dependent in some way on other earthly life, and in its turn contributes to other existences. This is the balance of nature, the circle of all living patterns on earth – the Circle of Life.

FEBRUARY 6TH
Our staff and rod

THE LIGHT OF SPIRIT

The streak of dawn peeps o'er the hill,
  To tell the night her task is done,
That God's own plan is working still,
  And darkness will be overcome.

This demonstration every morning,
  Renews our hopes for each new day,
For even as the sun is rising,
  This knowledge guides us on our way.

If we would know the power of Spirit,
  And use it for the good of Man,
We would see with each new dawning,
  The loving strength of Spirit's plan.

Rejoice all ye who glimpse the beauty,
  All who see the power of God,
All who know the path of duty,
  For you are blest with staff and rod.

And when another day is ending,
  And dusk is heralding the night,
Look towards the next dawn coming,
  Stand straight and tall towards the light.

★ ★ ★

FEBRUARY 7TH
Good medicine

A SMILE can heal a wound of the soul or soothe an aching heart. It can beam light into a shadow, or prompt another smile.

FEBRUARY 8TH
Giggle medicine

THE CURE

A giggle a day keeps the doctor away,
Or so my old granny once said,
But what do you do if laughs are too few,
And you're in bed with the 'flu and bad head?

You make up a rhyme to fill up the time,
And dance round the bedroom instead.
This remarkable trick will work very quick,
As you fall back again into bed.

For sleep will now come to cure anyone,
With the faith to write poems in bed,
Make sure they are funny, take plenty of honey,
And do what the doctor has said!

★ ★ ★

FEBRUARY 9TH
Compassionate medicine

VALUES

I saw a small child rushing round a Supermarket, picking up various items that caught his eye. He took these to his mother – "I want this" and "I want that," and his mother put them in her shopping trolley with a resigned expression – she looked too tired to think about it as she wandered amongst all the piles and piles of food, occasionally trying in a half hearted sort of way, to stop her child from making so much noise.

Later that day, I saw an item on television news – a small child with ribs that could be counted, a pot stomach that couldn't be missed and wide dark eyes that jerked my heart. This child of foreign war torn parts, held out a painfully thin arm in silent plea and thank you, as a voluntary worker from the west held out a morsel of food. Whatever has happened to our proper sense of values? The compassion and common sense with which we are all endowed is there – if we only care to use it.

32

FEBRUARY 10TH
A thought about sorrow

THE MEASURE OF GRIEF

When a life has run its earthly course, someone else is left to grieve the loss. The measure of that grief is dictated by the love that has been shared between the two, no other criterion can accurately assess the pain. Yet the parting is merely physical, and the love that has been shared remains the same, to give the same strength and loyalty that it has always known. This is true in every case of bereavement, whether the loss be relation or friend and whether the friend be human or pet animal.

★ ★ ★

FEBRUARY 11TH
It's so easy really

THE PERFECT GIFT

So many things cost such a lot –
Essential things of life,
But there is one without a price
That combats every strife.

It's free for everyone to use,
And makes our life worthwhile,
A present anyone can give –
This gift is called – a smile.

★ ★ ★

FEBRUARY 12TH
Shared opportunities

THE YOUNG IN YEARS have so much opportunity to build their stairway to the stars, older folk have so much opportunity to help them arrive safely.

33

THE PATH OF KINDLY FRIENDSHIP

The road to God is not the pomp and circumstance of worship,
Nor yet the gold and glitter set by man.
It is the woodland path of quiet friendship,
Where flowers of kindly deeds are God's own plan.

It is not the smooth and easy path to follow,
But twists and turns, with roots that make us stumble,
But God's own strength is there for us to borrow,
When prayer to Him is kind, sincere and humble.

And so the kindly deeds are heaven noticed,
In addition to our gratitude on earth,
And friendship links are thankfully accepted,
With the happiness that ever gives them birth.

Thus earthly time is coloured by your kindness,
Like God's own wild flowers along the way,
To lift a little of the world's own sadness,
And shine with peace and love in bright array.

★ ★ ★

LOVE IN THE MIST

That hardy pale blue annual of the traditional cottage garden, has defied all attempts to overcultivate or eradicate it – the fate of so many of our much loved garden flowers.

It is the namesake of traditional true love, that unexplainable, unselfish devotion that some people have always been able to give and accept, the love in a mist situation that defies all attempts to spoil it with a modern interpretation of love that is based on physical attraction only, and has no strength or roots to withstand the tests of time or adversity, whilst history can tell us of so many examples of true undying love that survive the mists of time and tribulation.

Some new things of the world are of great value, some of the older values are priceless and true love in the mist is one of them.

34

FEBRUARY 15TH
New love

SILENCE IS GOLDEN No. 2

They are talking and laughing as he tells her a joke about something that happened at work, when their eyes suddenly meet in a different way to the glances that they've known before. In spite of noise all around them, they share for a few moments – a silence that brings them together in a way that is new for them both – a recognition, they have fallen in love – a golden silence that will effect the rest of their lives.

★ ★ ★

FEBRUARY 16TH
Love lost in a giggle!

TIT FOR TAT

Did you ever see a mouse
   Tweaking a pussy tail?
For when there's a mouse about the house,
   Humour can never fail,
For pussy's temper doesn't rouse,
   When mousy fun sets sail,
She simply makes her pussy ve-ows
   To tweak a mousy tail!

★ ★ ★

FEBRUARY 17TH
A glorious opportunity

OUR HERITAGE

Birds are part of our heritage and we are part of theirs, and so we must learn to live together, sharing this planet with all its wonders and difficulties. We can make the world a glorious place for all the life that shares it, or we can destroy it with our ignorance and greed. Only mankind of earth's inhabitants wields this power, and so it is entirely up to us to guard these blessings.

FEBRUARY 18TH
A new fashion

COPYCATS

There is a strange little quirk of human nature that usually seems to go unnoticed – we are copycats! Any spectacular deed, whether it be good or bad, will find someone, somewhere trying to copy it, often to try and top it by making it worse, bigger, better, faster or crankier – depending on the nature of the act. The Guiness book of Records is full of such examples.

Even in ordinary everyday living, we copy fashions in so many things, clothes, hairstyles, cars, homes, sport, breeds of dogs, bathroom colours, garden planning, food and almost any other human activity of daily life that we can think of.

It therefore follows that a fashion for doing good and kindly deeds, should be fairly easy to promote, but although good things are done daily in their billions, we only seem to hear of a few isolated spectacular ones, and we can hardly claim "Good Works" to have been a fashion trend at any time in the history of Mankind. Perhaps there is little or no money in such activities, maybe it doesn't satisfy our egos. Modern newspaper, radio and television are not noted for making news items of the good and kindly acts that might inspire some copycats.

Perhaps it is time for a brand new fashion – smiles and good deeds everywhere we go, and a new slogan – "A kindness a day keeps the sadness at bay." All us copycats can have a wonderful time keeping up with the fashion, and really enjoy doing it. What a lot of sadness, fear and pain would be avoided.

Copycats could save the world and all humanity, if human beings would make it the latest fashion to copy all the best and kindest things in life.

★ ★ ★

FEBRUARY 19TH
A chance to grow

A KIND THOUGHT is the the embryo of good intention, but unless it is given the birth of human action, it can never be actually born and given the opportunity to grow on to maturity.

36

THE CHOICE

If a child is born with innocence
    Into a kindly family,
How is it that it can go wrong
    And express the traits of cruelty?

Perhaps it isn't born so pure,
    Maybe a memory survives
From another earlier time
    Of cruel and painful lives.

Perhaps its present life is giving
    Another noble chance,
For a soul to learn its lesson –
    To let compassion now advance.

Perhaps its present family
    Has been chosen for its caring,
Maybe true happiness is born
    With the kindly love and sharing.

Whichever way we look at life,
    It seems there's one thing certain,
The child is free to choose the depths,
    Or climb life's glorious mountain.

FEBRUARY 21ST
Love in disguise

COMPASSION is a gift of love.

37

A STORY OF FRIENDSHIP

Some think friendships grow on trees,
   Or offer it on bended knees.
Some think it just a game, and tease,
   Making friendship ill at ease.

Some people buy it in job lots,
   Or place it with Top Of The Pops.
To some it is Forget-me-nots,
   Or geraniums stuck in flower pots!

For friendship comes in many ways,
   With summer sun or winter days,
Springtime when the fledgling plays,
   Or sparked to life by autumn's grace.

And people have such strange ideas,
   Uncertain of their hopes and fears,
Breaking friendship's trust with tears,
   Till faith and courage reappears.

But we who know the truth indeed,
   And where to plant our friendship seed,
Know that love is friendship's creed,
   And know we can fulfil a need.

We know it comes from deep within,
   Cares not for things that might have been.
Love's future knows its way to win
   And further friendship's kith and kin.

We know it's tears and laughter too,
   We know it's friendship pure and true
When dawn of day brings love anew,
   And friendly love its thoughts pursue.

And so these friendly thoughts I leave,
   To grow from friendship's tiny seed
Planted when there was a need,
   To flower now, is truth indeed.

FEBRUARY 23RD
The time to count

THE RIGHT TIME

No matter how adverse our circumstances, there is always someone somewhere with an even greater burden. This is the right time to count our blessings – and there are always some of those as well. It is for us to recognise them.

★ ★ ★

FEBRUARY 24TH
Farewell to tears

THE PLEA

A baby's arms reach out in plea,
Its eyes are saying 'rescue me',
The need for this would never be
If people lived in harmony.

Each one of us can do our part
To make the tears and pain depart,
By living with a kindly heart,
We could make today the start.

The anxious times could disappear
If we would cast out want and fear,
And let compassion dry the tear
Through everyday of every year.

★ ★ ★

FEBRUARY 25TH
Our own efforts

OUR ACHIEVEMENTS

None of us can help being what we are according to our circumstances of birth, but our achievements – good or bad, small or large – are our own.

39

TORTOISE TALK

I know that we're slow,
But I want you to know
That our thoughts are both quiet and true,
For when spring comes around,
We'll make not a sound,
But we'll know straight away what to do!

Some eggs will be laid –
Though we're looking quite staid –
And they'll eventually turn into babies,
And soon they'll be found,
As we guide them around
The best lettuce and pretty lawn daisies.

It's easy to think
That we're not in the pink,
Because of the slow way we roam,
But never you fear
When opposition is near,
We can swiftly dive back in our home!

So don't be confused
When a low gear is used,
For high speeding may not do the job,
There are times when its safer
To just pray to your maker,
And get on with your task at a plod!

FEBRUARY 27TH
A painful thought

A MYSTERY

It is puzzling, that although most people do not like experiencing pain, many of those selfsame people actually enjoy inflicting it on others, perhaps in the name of sport, entertainment, commercial gain or even food. Others may not indulge in such action themselves, yet still condone it in other people. Both animals and fellow human beings can be the victims. It is a mystery that so many people seem unable to associate their personal ability to feel pain, with the suffering they inflict on other life. Perhaps they have forgotten that we reap as we sow – a fundamental fact of life.

A PRAYER FROM AN OLD ARMCHAIR

Please let me walk in a woodland,
   In mental attunement with trees,
Let me visualize green buds of springtime,
   And the flowers that the butterfly needs.

Please let me wander on pathways,
   In tune with the ringing blue haze
Of a glorious carpet of bluebells,
   I'll recall for the rest of my days.

May the pale gold of primrose enchant me,
   As it did when I walked long ago,
May those cushions of flowers ever rest me,
   As my memories and thoughts ebb and flow.

Please let my old memory wander
   With the birds that were fluttering there,
And the ferns that unfolded in beauty,
   Reaching out to the sweet woodland air.

Let me hear once again in my memory,
   The crack of a dry leaf and twig,
To rekindle the sound of the bird-song,
   And help reminiscing to live.

Please God let me find in your heaven,
   The woodlands I've known here on earth,
Perhaps with the special enchantment
   Of spiritual love and rebirth.

THE GUIDING LIGHT

Today comes but once in every four years, so its message must be a special one – "Let love be the guiding light of all life." It is the power to forgive and the source of compassion. Without it, all humanity would fail.

MARCH

WEST WINDS

MARCH 1ST
Sowing a harvest

MARCH

Could they but dare, the buds of March,
To stir beneath the dark tree bark,
And peep into the dawn of day,
For spring is not so far away,
And trees will clothe again in green
From those brown buds that were unseen.

Some daffodils begin to nod
Golden heads from soil untrod.
Biting March winds slope their stalks,
To sway and dance in ballet walks.
They catch the sunshine through the trees,
Give hope of summer, just to tease.

For summer sun is future still,
But tiny brown seeds, can and will
Produce our flowers and fruits of soil,
If March time is our planting toil.
For we must play our own true part,
To stir again the sleeping heart.

MARCH 2ND
An annual promise

THE COMING OF SPRING

See here the swelling leaf buds greet the spring,
White hoar-frost melts, revealing everything
The shining mantle has been sheltering,
And once again the birds begin to sing.

The winter aconite feels braver now
That greenish tips appear on every bough,
And primrose shows the promise of her vow
To clothe the banks and woodlands with her flower.

And we can see the power of God's hand,
Life's mystery in every grain of sand
That moulds the soil into a fertile land,
And stirs the coming spring at His command.

45

A HEAVENLY SPANK?

Said the parson to the choir boy,
  "Now you just look at me,
If you don't sing the hymns in tune,
  You'll make the angels flee.

And if you're misbehaving,
  While I lead the church in prayer,
Not only will the angels cry,
  But they'll spank your hide – so there!

And if you stick your chewing gum
  Underneath the seat,
I'll move it to the top my lad,
  And you'll be stuck there for a week.

So take that grin right off your face,
  And concentrate on prayer,
Remember Someone's watching you,
  And will know if you don't care.

And when you leave the choir stalls,
  Just keep it slow and quietly,
No winking at the girls you pass,
  Lest the angels haunt you nightly!"

★ ★ ★

MARCH 4TH
One little word

"BUT"

We've all had it said to us at sometime or other, and it has one of two possible meanings:– Either you don't want to hear it, or the speaker has a guilty conscience, maybe only slightly, but guilty just the same. The remark in question is "I hope you don't mind, but . . . " Isn't it strange how one little word can tell us much more than the speaker intends? !!!

THE GIFT OF SEASONS

When nature stirs the buds of spring
To bring new life to everything,
She clothes the trees with leafy green,
The finest gown you've ever seen
Sprinkled with flowers of gold and blue,
Mixed with every magic hue –
God's gift of springtime hope.

When nature spreads her summer glory,
To tell the world her splendid story
Of life in bloom to pure perfection,
Riots of colour for our selection,
From flame that's borrowed from the sun
To purest white the flowers come,
God's gift of summer splendour.

When nature drops her autumn leaves,
To toss them lightly on a breeze,
Drifting into hidden places,
With golden carpeting it graces
Every path in forest glade,
Dappled by the sun and shade,
God's gift of autumn glory.

When nature sleeps her winter days,
And jangling winds are songs of praise
Driving the snow in drifts of white,
To gleam and shine with the moon at night,
Peeping towards the spring ahead,
Reviving all that seemed so dead
God's gift of winter rest.

And so the seasons wend their way,
Through every year and every day,
Teaching people of the earth
The lessons of all life's rebirth,
Changing with the march of time
According to His laws sublime,
God's gift of endless life.

PROTECTION

The mists of time disguise events
That once took a leading role,
The memory blurs the sadder times
As protection for the soul.

But happier times will seem more bright
And given an extra glow,
Our memories know the kinder way –
God planned it to be so.

★ ★ ★

MARCH 7TH
A task for someone else

ILLOGICAL EATING

As the vast majority of people are born into this world without the instinct to kill, it follows that most of them would not eat meat if they first had to kill an animal in order to do so. Even dogs and many cats who have this basic instinct to kill for food – not too far back in their evolution, have lost the instinct to kill as they have become domesticated as pets. It is strange that although most human beings have also developed beyond any urge to kill, they will still eat meat, allowing someone else to do the killing for them.

★ ★ ★

MARCH 8TH
A task for wiser minds

HEAVEN'S HELP

If trouble strikes an unexpected blow,
And unseen forces knock you to and fro,
Remember there's another unseen power,
That wants to help you through that lonely hour.
You need not fight adversity alone,
For prayer will bring assistance winging home,
And you must use the help that is being given,
For wiser minds than ours can work in heaven
And know a better plan for us to follow,
Our trust in them can bring a bright tomorrow.

MARCH 9TH
A living message

A GENTLE THOUGHT

It's easy to be gentle
If your friends are gentle too,
Harder to be a gentle soul
If folks are harsh with you,
But God gives strength to kindness,
When a gentle soul is true
To the laws He made for living –
Old as time, yet ever new.

★ ★ ★

MARCH 10TH
An urgent message

A CLARION CALL

Triggered by our awareness of the need to conserve our environment, we realize at last that animals are a vital part of our own survival. The billions that have suffered and died for us and through us in the past, must not have suffered and died in vain. The bark in the wilderness is no longer just an appeal, it is a clarion call for courage and compassion in every corner of the earth to every thinking human being.

★ ★ ★

MARCH 11TH
A springtime message

A BREATH OF SPRING

A breath of spring – it's on its way,
To help us through another day,
A look to future love and healing
Gives everyday a brand new meaning,
For peace and courage of the mind
Gives sanctity of another kind –
The knowledge of all Spirit caring,
The springtime hopes we all are sharing,
And the love of Spirit never ending,
That's the joy that spring is lending.

49

MARCH 12TH
A caring message

PRIMROSES

There it sat – eight inches wide,
Shyly trying there to hide
In modesty among the leaves,
Beneath the overhanging trees.

A cushion filled with palest gold,
Such loveliness you will behold
To tease the mind in admiration,
For such a perfect gold creation.

This primrose plant just sitting there,
In beauty that she tries to share
With all her human being friends –
The message that our God intends.

Yet some are far too dull to see
The message there beneath the tree,
That when our gifts from God are shared,
They're doubled because somebody cared.

MARCH 13TH
Memory's message

THE SECRET GARDEN

Within the secret garden of my mind,
I treasure all the flowers of memory's time,
To live again with blossoms rare and fine –
A flower show of wondrous rich design.

Sometimes I wander through the garden gate,
To find the lovely flowers that friends create
Through passing years, regardless of their fate
They keep my secret garden up to date.

For memories old and new can here combine
To blossom in a fine display, and shine
With friendship's memories true and kind,
Enhance this secret garden that is mine.

50

PONDERINGS OF A GARDEN BIRD

It's nice to have these bushes here,
   To hide from next door's cat,
This garden's so untidy
   It's a treat and that's a fact,
For I can bob about all day
   Amongst the twigs and leaves,
To find the little slugs and things,
   And fallen flower seeds.
Everyday our breakfast comes,
   Tossed upon the lawn,
It's sometimes rather late I fear,
   'Cos I am up at dawn!
The nuts are nice all hanging there,
   And seed piled on a tray,
And when the bits of fat come out
   It's time to shout hooray!
No matter what the weather is,
   Or how the winds may blow,
Our human friends remember us,
   In rain or freezing snow.
There's lots of secret places here
   In which to build a nest,
From boxes, shrubs and garden shed,
   It's hard to know what's best.
I think I'll sing a special song
   For the owners of this garden,
To thank them for this wild place,
   That's such a birdie haven.

INSPIRATION

Different experiences provide inspiration for different people. A moment of inner knowledge for one person may mean nothing to another, and many look for such knowledge in wrong places. Usually the opportunity arrives unexpectedly, and it is for us to recognise and be aware of its value. Nature provides us with so many of these inspirational moments – the beauty and grace of the birds, their freedom and knowledge are sources of inspiration for those who are in tune with nature. With them our minds can fly towards the joy of living that God intended for us all.

MARCH 16TH
Progress

FORGIVING

It is easy to forgive someone you like or love if some little word or action from them disappoints. It is much harder to forgive a larger adversity or something that hurts our own pride or emotions. It is harder still to forgive someone we do not actually like very much. But spirituality of the mind can clear the pathway of all the obstacles that make it difficult for us to forgive, and success is true progress for the forgiving soul.

★ ★ ★

MARCH 17TH
A smile in the garden

'WEEDS'

How we gardeners hate them
As they invade our garden patch,
They've not been cultivated
And with our flowers they don't match.

Yet without them we would never know
Grand horticultural displays,
For these 'weeds' are the ancestors
From a long forgotten age.

So when we win a special prize
At our local flower show,
Let's not forget the wild flowers,
From which our prize blooms grow.

MARCH 18TH
Oneness with infinity

SILENCE IS GOLDEN No. 3

A quiet old country church – whilst other folk are eating their lunch or tea – a place where people have hoped, prayed and conversed with the angels and their God for hundreds of years. This is the golden silence of unseen strength that anyone may use, a oneness with infinity.

MARCH 19TH
The destination

THE JOURNEY TO PEACE OF MIND

Peace of mind is a precious gift to own, and yet it has to be earned. It is a destination of the soul, and roads must be travelled to reach it.

Some are the highways of major events, some are the quiet lanes of gentle thought and action. The vehicle in which to travel is the individual conscience, and some of those will be better serviced than others, but all can reach the destination safely if they are using the right map and read it well, for Peace of Mind stands out on a hilltop as an ultimate destination.

MARCH 20TH
Deep rooted faith

WEST WINDS

The west wind bends the Devon trees,
Driving in from Atlantic seas
To mould the stalwart trunks with ease,
Pointing their branches towards the east.

And yet the roots stay firm, and coil
Into Devon's fertile soil,
The west wind pits its strength and toil
In fruitless aim, the trees to foil.

The west winds tour a waiting world,
The warming breeze or gale unfurled
Against the western coastline hurled,
But jagged rocks stand undeterred.

The message of the trees is clear,
Stand firm in face of every fear,
Deep rooted faith be brought to bear
Against life's west wind's wear and tear.

53

MARCH 21ST
Springtime inspiration

THE CHOIR

If music be the song of life,
     Then bird-song is the choir,
For the springtime dawning chorus,
     Is the perpetuating fire
That leads the birds to loving,
     And the nestlings they desire.
This sheer simplicity of life
     We surely must admire,
For the tireless work and artistry,
     And the courage they acquire.
Let the message of the bird-song
     Our human hearts inspire.

MARCH 22ND
A glance back

THE MINOR UNEXPECTED HAPPENING so often becomes something of importance in our lives, its value only recognised by hindsight.

MARCH 23RD
Give and take

THE CHANCE TO CARE

If no-one ever suffered
     In this old world of ours,
Kindness could not ever grow,
     And blossom as God's flowers.

And so the human race would fade
     For want of kindly action,
If no-one had the chance to care,
     Life's purpose wouldn't function.

The balance of the master plan
     For every single soul,
Is a partnership of give and take
     Towards a heavenly goal.

A GOOD IDEA

The older mind seems far behind
  So many new inventions,
But experience can lend a hand,
  Backed up by good intentions.

If young and old would blend and mould
  Their knowledge and their fears,
The world could be an easier place
  As it travels through the years.

For new things take us forward,
  Old knowledge steers a course,
This sharing is a partnership
  That creates success at last.

MARCH 25TH
Listening ears

THE VOICE OF THE CHILDREN

Children play, they squeal, shriek and shout in sheer delight, while others scream in temper and frustration. Even the gentler moments of quiet chatter are part of the noise that healthy children make. But the voices of the young can overwhelm not only the older generation, but the whimper of children in distress, the despairing cry of hopelessness, the silent cry of appealing eyes that know no hope but the presence of an adult, who may or may not care, for some of these will help whilst others will betray the trusting appeal cast in their direction.

This betrayal can be found in many parts of the world – among the man-made wars, the streets of poverty and comfortable homes of civilization where a lonely abused child knows no other way of life.

Many people hear the voice of childish appeal, too few take much notice or let conscience prompt an action. For some children the quiet whimper or silent look of despair are their only hope. Let not the cacophony of noise of happy children disguise the voices of despair.

MARCH 26TH
Some friendly thoughts

FLOWERS OF KINDNESS

When kindness reaches out a helping hand
Towards a lonely soul in deep distress,
It says "Dear friend, I really understand,"
And offers peace of mind and quiet rest.

When a word is gently floated on the air,
To soothe the turmoil of a troubled mind,
It says "Dear friend, there's someone here to care,
That happiness one day you'll really find."

When a smile is beamed towards another soul,
Where smiling seems to be a foreign part,
It says "Dear friend, I'll help you gain control
Of the sadness lingering there within your heart."

When a dream is offered to a weakened will,
To chase the shadows from a lonely life,
It says "Dear friend, I'll travel with you still,
To help you overcome the toil and strife."

When love is reaching out with good intent,
Unselfish in its purpose and its plan,
It says "Dear friend, my help is truly meant,"
For sincerity will always understand.

So if your heart is laden down with sorrow,
Accept the kindly help that comes your way,
It says "Dear friend, I'll brighten your tomorrow
With flowers of kindness blossoming today."

MARCH 27TH
Disguise

SELF DECEPTION

When a truth has been firmly established in our minds, it cannot be removed. It
can however be disguised when we don't wish to acknowledge its presence, but
this entails being dishonest with ourselves.

MARCH 28TH
Outside our control

WEATHER-WISE

"It's raining again." "Phew, it's too hot." "Brr, it's jolly cold." "I wish the wind would drop." We are never satisfied are we? But without rain we would have no food or flowers. Without sun we would have darkness and nothing could survive. The frost kills off germs and breaks up lumpy soil, and the winds prune out dead branches from our trees and help to dry out wet places where they should not be.

Thank heaven there is a wiser mind than ours to control the elements. At least human discord and difference of opinion cannot cause a war about that particular subject!

★ ★ ★

MARCH 29TH
A smile and flick of a tail

SQUIRREL SENSE

There are lots of funny folk about,
　For some say that I'm a rat,
But with a bushy tail like mine,
　I'm more like a Persian cat!

But cats don't eat the nuts and fruit
　That are my staple diet,
So I think that Squirrel is my name,
　And further more – I'll prove it.

For I can climb up anything
　Much faster than they can,
And I can leap from tree to tree
　With an enormous span.

Rats and cats are carnivores,
　My food is so much kinder,
But it's true I'll eat an egg or two
　Just to make my menu wider.

But I'll not scratch your best armchair,
　Or gnaw holes in your doors,
I'll just amuse you for a while,
　Holding nuts between my paws.

I hope you have no further doubts,
　For this matter is quite trivial,
As with this flicking bushy tail
　I'm obviously a squirrel!

THE MARCH OF TIME

There is so much of it – time, that we often do not value it as we should. We waste it, misuse it and so often fail to share or give it to others as we could. It is only with our own advancing years – as time marches relentlessly onwards that we realise the many better ways that we could have used some of our earlier time.

Time unwisely spent cannot be recalled, but it can still serve as guidance for the time that is now, or is still in future days. Our own past experiences could even guide a younger life if they would spare the time to listen and reflect on the experiences of those who have already known, enjoyed or regretted so much of their own past times. The march of time has no rules but its own relentless rhythm, it is for us to do the best we can with it whatever our age may be.

★ ★ ★

MARCH 31ST
The pattern of life

LIFE CONTINUOUS

A field of golden daffodils, nodding in the breeze,
Clumps of gentle primrose at the feet of woodland trees.
Bluebells ringing out their tune,
Rising quickly, gone too soon.
But they appear again next year,
Still free of sorrow, hate or fear.
We too survive the season death
To brighten someone's sleeping breath,
Here on earth or heavenly plane,
Like flowers of truth – we live again,
Continuous as the night and day,
Our spirits wend their happy way
Towards that perfect, glorious land.
Help all you can, stretch out your hand,
That others find a peace to bless,
In trees and flowers and happiness.

APRIL

WILD SPRING FLOWERS

APRIL 1ST
Springtime

APRIL

The primrose shyly peeping now
Beneath the fern fronds curve unfurled.
April violets scent the airflow,
Amongst the hedgerow leaves uncurled.

The glinting gold of daffodils
Puts to shame the miser's hoard.
Springtime promise still fulfils
The prayer of souls throughout the world.

APRIL 2ND
Shared humour

THE FUNNY SIDE

Happiness is not laughter at someone else's expense, but a sharing of the funny side of life that lurks behind all kinds of adversity.

APRIL 3RD
Some hidden blessing

TRUTH

Blest are those with the eyes to see
The rivers of truth that are flowing free,
Blest are those with the ears to hear
The wisdom of truth that casts out fear.
Blest are the minds that can understand
That the truth of love is a helping hand,
And blest are the souls that follow the path
Of a truthful mind and a kindly heart.

61

THE HEDGEHOG

Please don't disturb, I'm half awake
    From my winter sleep,
It's been so cosy curled up here
    Beneath your compost heap.

If you are very nice to me,
    I'll use my eating powers,
And get to work on slugs and things,
    To save your lovely flowers.

I'll do my very best for you,
    Lest I should get the sack,
I'll help you find a smile or two
    With an apple on my back!

But when the summer's ended,
    And I've cleared most of the grubs,
I'd be grateful for some doggie food
    To supplement the slugs!

Then I'll curl into a ball again,
    All nice and fat and round,
To sleep beneath your compost heap,
    All nice and safe and sound.

So please remember I am here,
    Keep your garden fork at bay,
Those spikes would be such nasty things
    If they should stray my way.

And when the spring comes round again,
    You will surely see
Your friend the hedgehog running round –
    It's back to work for me!

But you my friend can rest awhile,
    Put away the pesticide,
'Cos I'll be ready for the fray,
    With nature on my side.

You are there

A FRIEND INDEED

When life is turning upside-down,
    And no-one understands,
When my brow can only frown,
    And I'm needing helping hands,
And life is shades of grey and brown –
    This isn't how I'd planned.

I tried so hard to bear my load
    Alone and unafraid,
But life was such a rocky road,
    And God seemed far away.
But then I prayed that friends I'd made
    Would around me stay.

Then suddenly, an answered prayer –
    A solace to my need,
A gentle touch that says "I care,"
    And loving eyes that plead.
My dog is there, my life to share,
    I have a friend indeed.

★ ★ ★

APRIL 6TH
Economy

JUST ONE KIND WORD serves a greater purpose than any number of words said in anger – a great economy of words and time.

★ ★ ★

APRIL 7TH
Seasonal gifts

SPRINGTIME SHARING

A breath of spring – it's on its way,
To help us through another day,
A look to future love and healing
Gives everyday a brand new meaning,
For peace and courage of the mind,
Gives sanctity of another kind,
The knowledge of all Spirit caring,
The springtime hopes we all are sharing,
The love of Spirit never ending,
That's the joy that spring is lending.

APRIL 8TH
Spring magic

WILD SPRING FLOWERS

The ringing sound of blue bells
  Reflects their gentle blue,
The message that they truly tell
  Are Spirit's perfect hues.

The modest sighs of primrose,
  Nestled with the ferns,
Lifting a smile on tip toes,
  As they greet the spring's return.

The golden stars of celandine,
  Brighten the path ahead,
Such glory will be truly seen
  When a spiritual life is led.

The magic of the springtime,
  With promise all aglow,
Is the knowledge of a lifetime
  Lent for us to know.

But if the wild sounds evade you,
  And you cannot tune your ear,
Just be thankful for the life that's new,
  That you can see and hear.

APRIL 9TH
A partnership

SONS OF THE SOIL

Those who work the soil, see the beauty and natural things of life with a different eye to most other people. They appreciate the majesty of fine old trees and grand landscapes, and at the same time value the very soil from which they come, as they rely upon these things for their livelihood. They need to work in partnership with nature and not against her as so many other folk try to do. A true son of the soil understands the balance that must be maintained, and this knowledge guides towards greater spirituality, whether or not it is recognised as such.

THE LADY

She lived in name and action of her kind,
She came this way, and journeyed on again,
Her mark was written in the sands of time,
As kindly deeds and heaven's true compassion.
This lady with the gift of gracious loving,
Paused in life to help the injured mouse,
And lifted up a lonely child crying,
As she gazed with longing eyes for heaven's help.

If pain was part of life and daily living,
It was the grief for others that she bore,
For this lady of the gentle smile and giving,
Walked a path where too few have walked before.
If anger slipped between those lips unbidden,
It was in sorrow for another's fear or pain,
For she could see the light of peace tomorrow,
And wished that all the world could do the same.

I remember now the smile of gentle kindness,
The understanding touch for those in need,
For both animals and people were her giving,
She, the enemy of cruelty and greed.
This lady of the loving thought and action,
Has journeyed on to help the angels sing,
But you can find her friends if you keep looking,
For her legacy of love will never end.

HEAVEN'S BLENDING

The mighty power of spirit lending
  Loving strength to Mother Earth,
Brings earth and heaven's timely blending
  To teach the world true loving's worth,
For therein lies the art living
  With love and faith through earthly birth.
This is the knowledge never ending,
  This is the secret of heaven's truth.

APRIL 12TH
A clearer view

HINDSIGHT

Advancing years give the advantage of hindsight, it becomes easier to judge ourselves. Our words, actions and motives all become clearer as we look back. There will be some regrets, some pleasure and satisfaction with our efforts through the years. We cannot alter or correct the regrets, but we can still do something to redress the balance of earlier mistakes. If we do this and learn by our errors, we shall not have lived in vain.

★ ★ ★

APRIL 13TH
A giggle day.

HAT CAT

I feel a pretty silly cat,
Wearing a flower for a hat,
But people smile at such silly things,
And so to please – some fun I brings –
A smile to please my human friends,
'Cos happiness on a smile depends!

★ ★ ★

APRIL 14TH
After the storm.

SILENCE IS GOLDEN No. 4

Before a thunder storm, there is a curious woolly silence that will contrast sharply with the cacophony of noise that follows. And when the thunder and lightning have died away with ever decreasing strength, we are left with a clear bright silence – golden moments of peaceful, clarified air.

★ ★ ★

APRIL 15TH
A special strength

PATIENCE is a silent strength of mind.

66

THE GIFT OF SPRING

Spring in the woods amongst the trees,
Spring in the garden with fresh green leaves,
The primrose flower that seeks to please,
The spirit of spring that will buzz with bees
And lift our hearts on a gentle breeze,
For God in His mercy has given us these,
To give the world a glimpse of peace.

BIRTH OF LIFE

The roots of life are deep within
    The very soul of man,
The leaves of life spring forth from roots
    Propelling the greater plan.
And after leaves, the flowers spring
    The opportunities of life,
Some will form a sweet bouquet,
    Whilst others fade with strife.
But those that live will bear the fruits
    Nurtured with loving care,
To feed the very soul of man
    That brought the fruit to bear.
The circle of all life responds
    To thinking that is right,
Born of truth and sincerity
    Upon the wings of light.
And when mankind has learnt the rules
    Of nature's faultless plan,
He too can live in the glorious truth
    That was there since the world began.

★ ★ ★

A FROWN makes everyone else frown, a smile makes at least some of them smile as well!

APRIL 19TH
A journey to maturity

NOBILITY

Such sovereignty, such majesty,
  Symbol of a greater destiny,
Such strength to lend humanity –
  An integral part of history.

There's protection in its noble spread,
  In the beauty of its royal head,
The food it gives, the soil to feed,
  All of these fulfil a need.

Its mystic power the heavens invoke,
  To tell if rain will splash or soak,
Through a hundred years of power and growth,
  From acorn seed to mighty oak.

APRIL 20TH
A desirable possession

TOO MUCH AND TOO LITTLE

Greediness is probably the single greatest cause of unhappiness the world over. Its cause and effect is not only experienced by the human race, animals are often the victims and will also exhibit this undesirable trait themselves, although in their case it is likely to be part of their instinctive survival mechanism, because their greed is usually associated with food.

No such excuse can be found for most people. Too many of them want more of so many things, when in fact they already have more than enough to satisfy their needs. In addition to money we find greed entering the realms of quite ordinary everyday possessions and positions in life. Whilst large portions of the world's population are short of the bare necessities of life, other people elsewhere have a surfeit of even luxury items, yet fail to share their good fortune – that is greed.

Thankfully there are many people who set a finer example of life, sometimes they are folk who do not have very much themselves, thus generosity is all the greater, and it is this that should stir the conscience of the greedy, for in giving they receive and find true happiness, surely a very desirable possession for everyone.

APRIL 21ST
Supreme links

THE DAISY CHAIN

The daisy is a simple flower
But its message is supreme,
For every flower speaks of life,
And all life speaks of God,
God teaches us the power of love,
And love could save the world.

APRIL 22ND
Squatters

CUCKOO

The cuckoo is one of our most popular wild birds. It heralds the coming summer days and so uplifts our thoughts, telling us that winter is well and truly behind us. Its cheerful call is so distinctive that we can't fail to recognise it, even though an occasional human cuckoo tries to emulate it just for fun, which only emphasises our light-hearted attitude to this bird of woodland trees and early summer days.

However, cuckoos do have another less attractive side to them, for they employ a sort of Ornithological Squatters Rights system for bringing up their young, a single egg in someone else's nest when the rightful owner isn't looking. As the egg often resembles those already in occupation, the resident parents don't seem to know the difference. When the eggs hatch, this delinquent child of the cuckoo proceeds to turf out the residential offspring who are much smaller anyway, and the foster parents are left to bring up this single intruder as best they may, their own babies having died either from a crash landing beneath the nest or from lack of food or warmth.

As something like ten nests can be violated in this way, it is clear that this vagabond of the bird world has much to answer for, and it is a curious thought that we have to tolerate having people amongst us who behave in equally irresponsible, selfish and brutal ways. There would seem to be only two significant differences between the two miscreants, the human ones should know better, and they don't even possess the charm of the bird that at least brings us good news, whilst the human variety is bad news by anybody's reckoning! It is amazing how much we can learn from nature, perhaps we'd all go cuckoo if we didn't!

APRIL 23RD
The perfect recipe

FRIENDSHIP PIE

Mix together equal quantities of faith, hope and charity, season well with tolerance and understanding. Place in a well greased non-stick pan, and cover with a thick pastry of trust. Bake in a moderate heat of generosity and serve with liberal portions of cream of unselfishness. There is no need to add love as this recipe creates that ingredient during preparation. This dish will keep indefinitely under any circumstances. Warning – share this pie only with people you really know and care about, others may find it too rich and indigestible!

APRIL 24TH
Turning the tables with a smile

CHILDREN

Children can be such a blessing,
  Also a pain in the neck,
Their funny remarks so refreshing,
  But their actions can cause quite a wreck.

The innocent smile of a baby
  Jerks the heart of a cynical man,
But later the mischief comes daily,
  And worse, it's according to plan!

We worry and laugh through their school days,
  Teenage time seems to be even worse,
Till the hair on our heads turns to multiple greys,
  And it's *their* turn to worry for us!

APRIL 25TH
Sorting out the lazy bones!

WHO'S TOO BUSY?

If you need help for something important, ask a busy person – they will somehow find the necessary time. Other people won't bother to look.

THE UNHEARD VOICES

If lambs and pigs could talk to us,
    And cows give their ideas,
Would they demand cold concrete pens
    Or tags pierced through their ears?

If baby chicks could cheep their wish
    For a contented pain free life,
Would they really choose a crowded cage
    That gives them naught but strife?

If horses, calves and wild game
    Could tell us what they think,
And turkeys gobble out their views,
    Could we with them link?

If the animals could state their case,
    It would surely be a plea,
Against the cruel way they live,
    When they really should be free.

If the animals could voice their fear
    Of slaughter and the smell of blood,
Who would dare to strike the blow,
    Simply for needless food?

If the animals could talk to us,
    They might request a kindly thought
For compassion in our daily lives,
    Just as the Master taught.

If people then would spare a thought
    That the killing and pain can cease,
Mankind could walk with head held high,
    And find his conscience filled with peace.

★ ★ ★

THE MAJOR ERROR

Greed is the one overriding sin of mankind, for it is the root cause of all other errors.

71

APRIL 28TH
A blessing

FRIENDSHIP'S FOUNDATION

With friendships built on love and trust,
Defying every test and thrust
Of earthly time and situation,
Knowing well its own creation,
It learns the secret of success,
And gently knows it's truly blest.

APRIL 29TH
Swords, bombs and money

PROGRESS?

Sadly, it is a fact of life that opponents of almost any project good or bad can be
overcome if they can be hit in their pocket. Perhaps this can even be called
progress, because it *must* be an improvement on the ancient use of the sword or
modern practice of hitting with a bullet or bomb, but there must surely be a
more spiritual path between.

APRIL 30TH
There's one for everyone

SOME THOUGHTS ABOUT PRAYER

A prayer said at morning
    Brings new hope with the dawning,
A prayer for each day
    Helps keep evil away,
A prayer said at night
    Helps keep everything right,
A prayer from the soul
    Helps keep everything whole,
A prayer that's sincere
    Keeps our consciences clear,
But a prayer put in action
    Is our finest reaction,
So that our prayers become service
    With God's strength to uphold us.

MAY

NATURE'S HEALING PEACE

MAY 1ST
Almost summer

MAY

The month of May – she charms us still,
The bright fresh days will yet fulfil
Our hopes of sunshine's warming thrill,
And the soaring skylark's joyous trill,
For summer is nearly here.

The hawthorn proudly now displays
Her scented dress of bygone days,
Renewed again by nature's ways,
And hides the fledgling as she plays,
And knows that summer's here.

Bluebells nod their graceful heads,
Hyacinths rise from well planned beds
And lawn mowers trundle from their sheds,
To neaten where a lady treads
Now that summer's here.

Hope is high in the month of May,
Some glory has been – yet passed away,
But there's much more for a later day.
So lift your thoughts to God and pray,
With thanks that May is here.

MAY 2ND
Wisdom

COMMON SENSE

"Use Your Common Sense" – easy advice to give, not always so easy to follow, for common sense needs also to be good sense, which is not nearly as common as we would like to believe. As common sense is basically the wise use of any knowledge we may have acquired through time, it seems that some people learn quicker than others, for we can see a young child displaying greater sense than some adults. Perhaps these younger wise ones have brought knowledge to earth with them from a previous existence or were diligent scholars in their 'heavenly' state before they were born into this particular era. Whatever the explanation, the rest of us would do well to note their knowledge and their wisdom in using it.

THE FUSSY BUTTERFLY

I'm just a little butterfly
Looking out for mischief,
I very often wonder why
I was born inquisitive.

I poke my nose in pretty flowers,
To see what I can find,
I flit around for many hours
To find the nicest kind.

Ah, here's a petal that is new,
I'll see what here reposes,
It's got a most peculiar pooh –
I think I'll stick to roses!

★ ★ ★

MAY 4TH
A master plan

SUMMER IS ON ITS WAY

The hush that heralds summer's sultry day,
Hovers in the air not far away.
The gentle rains that fall begin to say,
Summer flowers will bloom with bright array.

Nesting birds have flitted to and fro,
Fluttering offspring follow where they go.
Nature now will leap to summer's glow,
The master plan dictates it will be so.

Anticipation of the summer sun,
Long days of toil and happy joyful fun,
With summer flowers and fruit for everyone,
Demands a prayer of thanks when day is done.

Blest are the sounds of summer's golden ray,
As bird-song greets another new-born day
Lambs will run and gambol in their play,
And we will know that summer's on its way.

THE WILLING PUPIL

Everyday of our lives has something worthwhile to teach us – it is we who must be willing to learn!

★ ★ ★

MAY 6TH
A friendly truth

FRIENDSHIP LINKS

True friendship's links are ties that bind
Not with rope or hoops of steel,
But silken threads which you will find,
Soft as gossamer they feel.

Every friendship runs its life,
Has its purpose to fulfil,
Through happiness or tinged with strife,
True friendship grows on still.

Each friendship has its weight and strength,
Like ships upon the sea.
Each friendship lives its total length,
Its span is meant to be.

No true friendship can be lost,
However brief its stay.
Some upon the seas are tossed,
Some in calmer waters lay.

True friendship always knows its time
To greet the ebb and flow.
For God's own plan is love divine,
And always will be so.

★ ★ ★

MAY 7TH
Good sense

OPTIMISM is positive thinking towards any desired results. It can most certainly work, so it is important to make sure that the desired result is a good one – in every sense of the word.

THE MAGIC BLACKBIRD

I hear you magic blackbird
　From your blossomed bough,
My sleek and lovely songbird,
　Your trills are praises now
That lift towards your maker
　In gratitude for life,
And nature's own creator
　Accepts your song of love.

I see you magic blackbird
　Defend your territory,
I watch you lovely songbird
　Rise up with majesty,
For the younger life that follows
　Under your protecting wing,
Will also know the sorrows
　That life on earth can bring.

I love you magic blackbird,
　Your courage is supreme,
I'll tell you lovely songbird,
　Of my secret dream.
I'd fly with you to heaven,
　Singing all the way,
That man finds God is proven,
　And God may hear me pray.

MAY 9TH
A courageous thought

THE DETERMINATION OF COURAGE

Courage comes in many guises, perhaps by bearing long illness or disability with dignity and grace, or speaking out in a right cause when others fail to whisper.

It can manifest in quiet perseverance against tremendous odds or forge an unchartered course through unknown terrains of land, sea, space and thinking. Some risk or give their lives to save another life under arduous physical threat, there is no end to the ways in which courage can appear, but all have two things in common, a clear cut knowledge of what is right and a magnificent determination to overcome adversity. The angels smile on such as these, and lend their own helping hands.

78

A smile with a message

A MOTORIST'S DREAM

The road is straight, no twists or bends,
   And half a mile wide,
A car in front that can be passed
   With a dash from either side.

With revving throttle's roaring sound
   Tempting a driver's fate,
He knows that he can stop of course
   Before it is too late.

With flights of fancy, dashing on,
   Filled with unseen power,
Eating up those puny miles
   At ninety miles an hour.

That crawling car is in the way,
   The driver looks quite shifty,
He's a danger on the road,
   He's only doing fifty.

The road is safe, just made for speed,
   Till a mirage is espied,
Some idiot has planted trees,
   Or perhaps the road map lied.

Drunk with speed and engine power,
   Illusion now takes hold,
What's this slowcoach doing here,
   That car is far too old.

It feels the car has sprouted wings
   And is very close to flying,
No danger in this world of speed,
   No thought or risk of dying.

It's riding high this driver's dream,
   It cannot hesitate,
Until the driver sees ahead –
   A shining Pearly Gate.

Generous knowledge

BLEST are those with the knowledge of unselfish love and give it freely.

DAISIES

A daisy can be big and bold
  To grace the flower border,
But some are very small indeed –
  Are of a lower order.

Some call them weeds upon the lawn,
  And think they have no right
To blossom there in bright array,
  A dream of dappled white.

It would be a dreadful thought
  To judge people in this way,
The grand would burst with self esteem,
  While the humble could only pray.

And yet these flowers are the same
  As the Daisy Grandiflora,
God's pattern is the same for both,
  It's just the size that He did alter.

The daisy proves a fact of life,
  That all can play their part
To make the world a brighter place,
  With a happy, sunny heart.

THE FOOD OF LOVE

If working be the bread of life,
  And conversation be the drink,
With bird-song for the joys we need,
  And pain to make us think,
Then laughter is the food of love
  To make our days complete.

MAY 14TH
A walk with God

NATURE'S HEALING PEACE

If I could walk down by the river,
   And hear its soft bubbling song,
I'd watch as it tumbles so whitely
   Over rocks as it flows gently on.

And then I'd find time for to wander
   Through springtime's own green woodland way,
Last year's beech leaves would flutter and rustle,
   And I'd wonder what they're trying to say.

Primrose vale is the path I would follow,
   With its cushions of pure palest gold,
To find the true joy of a bluebell dell,
   Misty carpet of blue to behold.

I'd carefully step through these flowers of spring
   'Neath cathedral arches of trees,
The songs of the birds play the music,
   With the murmur of hundreds of bees.

When I walk on down by the river,
   And find all these beautiful things,
I'll know I am walking with God at my side,
   And the sweet healing peace that it brings.

MAY 15TH
Pure silence

SILENCE IS GOLDEN No 5

Many of our waterways are busy with commercial or leisure activities, but here and there are lonely stretches of water that are peopled only by water wildlife, mystery and birds. Some such spots of sanctity can be found on the Norfolk Broads, conserved with diligence and devotion by those who understand its value and message.

To take a punt across a stretch of water such as this – the quiet peace broken only by the drips of water from the punt pole, creates a oneness with the universe. As you drift across the water, you can hear the silence of purity – awareness from the soul. This is the perfect golden silence that will be remembered for the rest of your life and beyond.

THE HEALING DAWN

The night-time blessings greet the light
   Of every new-born day.
The night-time stars slip out of sight
   As blackbird stirs his lay.

A morning glow slips o'er the hill,
   To shine in bright array,
And all the world is hushed and still
   To greet the coming day.

With every morning born anew,
   Comes loving hope and healing.
The freshly falling morning dew,
   Perpetuates the gleaning.

The clarity of morning rays,
   Heals the soul that's torn
With sorrows of sad yesterdays,
   To shine again with dawn.

The passing of another day,
   Will cloud sad memories,
Bid them fade and fly away,
   With the healing dawn tomorrow.

A WOOLLY LAMB

If we let a young child cuddle and play with a real live woolly lamb, who would dare take it away from the child and explain that you are going to kill it to eat it? For that matter who would dare kill it anyway?

    There are times when a child's innocence gets nearer to God's truth than all our sophisticated adulthood.

A PRAYER FOR KINDNESS

Oh Spirit of all light and love,
   Please hear my anxious prayer,
That people gathered on the earth,
   May learn to love and care
For those who suffer in this world
   In sorrow, everywhere.

May the love of Spirit guidance,
   Lift all these aching hearts,
And soothe the pain man is inflicting,
   Send the love that God imparts
To every corner of the earth,
   That man may find God's truth at last.

May kindness be a part of living,
   Reaching out to every life,
To every soul that cries in torment,
   To ease the pain and clear all strife.
Oh Spirit of all love and power,
   Please help us see Thy Light.

May the peoples of our earth plane,
   Be conscious of this crying need
For compassion never ending,
   May they learn to sow the seed
Of kindness, in their every action,
   That it may flower in every deed.

Oh Spirit of all light and love,
   Please help us find the way
To learn and teach compassion's truth,
   Through each and everyday,
That we reveal the love of God
   In all we do and say.

Please may we find His greatest blessing
   In peace throughout our world,
Because we've learnt God's wondrous lesson
   As His compassion is revealed.
Please show us how to live that message,
   As love and kindness are unfurled.

MAY 19TH
A tree necessity

OUR FRIENDS THE TREES

Trees are such a vital part of the world's life chain, that it is quite extraordinary that mankind should treat them so carelessly and selfishly, for it is against all common sense and loyalty to behave towards our friends in such a way.

In the very early days of mankind's evolution, the trees were revered often to the point of worship. Without actual scientific knowledge such as we have today, it is clear that the people of those times had an instinctive knowledge of the value of trees to their lives. It was not until much later that mankind began to massacre the tree population for his own material purposes. Once it was realised that the felling of trees for manufacturing purposes was a profitable occupation, it did not take long for the wholesale slaughter of trees to come about, as mankind's inherent greed took over, and in many areas still exists today, in spite of the more enlightened efforts of many people and organisations to halt the killing.

Trees are not only beautiful to look at, they clean our air by oxygenating it, they stabilize the soil with their roots, fertilize it with their leaves and provide efficient wind brakes to prevent its erosion. In addition to these basic services to mankind, trees provide homes and shelter for nearly all our animal wildlife, food for many of them including the human species. They even give us some herbal medicines to cure our ills.

We have used trees also for many basic material needs, such as tables and chairs, ships and farming equipment. Only mankind's greed and tendency to overpopulate the environment brought the wood of trees into greater demand than the tree population could sustain.

We wouldn't dream of treating our human friends in this way, and most of us wouldn't treat animal friends in such an illogical and irresponsible manner either, so why on earth do we treat our friends the trees so badly?

★ ★ ★

MAY 20TH
A special gift

CANINE DEVOTION

The devotion of a dog is its special unselfish gift to all humanity.

MAY 21ST
Different smiles

A SENSE OF HUMOUR – That indispensable piece of personal equipment that can see us through many a crisis, lift another unhappy soul, and make a friend. It can be shared with both pets and people.

Like everything else, it also has its negative side, for laughter for the wrong reason can hurt another – both mentally and physically. The cruel jibes of sardonic wit, many a practical 'joke', poking fun from a superior position – all examples of destructive humour – denote a low standard of spirituality and thinking, and with these we can easily *lose* a friend.

The problem with our sense of humour, is that it varies so much from person to person. Like honesty, integrity and kindness, we have different ideas and standards for our humour. To fully appreciate this particular gift, we need a good imagination. To use it well and wisely, we need common sense and a kindly disposition.

★ ★ ★

MAY 22ND
Giggle nonsense?

OTHER POINTS OF VIEW

Wouldn't it be comical
   If people could be fleas?
And fleas could change to human beings
   And live a life of ease?

No need to sort out someone's cat,
   Or jump about in beds,
They'd simply use a microwave
   When they wanted to be fed.

How very aggravating
   To be turned into a flea,
So that when you're feeling hungry,
   You have to find a juicy knee!

It's hard to walk in another's shoes
   To find their point of view,
And thankfully we have no need
   To know what a flea would do!

There could be other times of course,
   When it would be very wise
To see the different angle
   Of other people's lives!

85

THE MYSTERY OF FRIENDSHIP

Friendship is a strange relationship that is difficult to define, because it means so many different things to different people. A friendship to one person may be only an acquaintanceship to another. For some, friendship is a round of parties, sports or other social events, whilst others recognise it in a oneness of thought – an unexplainable link that draws hearts and minds together almost as if they are two parts of one whole. This quality can be found within a marriage, between brothers and sisters or two complete strangers that have been brought together with friendship in some mysterious way that defies ordinary explanation. Most friends of this calibre can look back on a strange set of coincidences that culminated in their meeting and the opportunity for true friendship – a 'Meant To Be' situation.

Perhaps they have known each other before in a previous life, or maybe it is the start of something new that is also meant to be. Whatever the explanation, it is a wise soul that recognises the situation sufficiently to take that opportunity to build a treasured friendship. The opportunity may not be followed up by reasoned or logical thinking with the superficial mind, for in such a case it would more likely be an inner knowledge, a soul's choice of recognition. The quality of such a friendship is quite beyond description for those who are privileged to share it. There are so many shades of friendship.

Animals too can share a close understanding that can only be described as friendship. It can be between two animals or between an animal and human companion. It can be on an acquaintanceship level or that deeper oneness of mind that we can recognise between two people. Dogs in particular can develop a selfless devotion that would put many a human relationship to shame. Dogs and horses have been known to become aware of a close friend being in danger, although they may be physically miles apart, just as human friends can collect the knowledge of such situations, apparently from thin air.

In the absence of any reliable explanation or label, we can only call it friendship, leaving the individual to take their own meaning from a very open ended word – one that is often misused, frequently underestimated, and truly understood by a privileged few. It is sometimes taken for granted, yet it is appreciated by so many, and its value is beyond price – the mystery of friendship.

BOYS OF TWO

What is it about a boy that tugs at mother's heart-strings?
Although he clutters up the home with all his toys and playthings?
Why is it that his tears and smiles can melt a stalwart heart,
And turn Mum's "No" to Father's "Yes" – and tear the home apart?
What is it that blinds our eye to every naughty trick,
When he stamps his foot, pouts his lip or pokes us with a stick?
How *does* he look so innocent, so quiet and so frail,
When he hits the cat, tips up our tea and pulls the pet dog's tail?
Mother doesn't know the reason, she's too kind to see the ploy,
But *he* knows very well you see, the advantage of being a boy.
He knows he can win every time he smiles,
His age of two keeps smiling through for ninety years of wiles,
And as he grows with passing years, other hearts will flutter,
But mother saw it first and knew the truth of such a matter.
For boys can't keep such secrets, their thoughts are open wide,
As they charge on, with yells and shouts and proper manly pride.

★ ★ ★

GIRLS OF TWO

Tossing curls and flashing eyes, with demurely fluttering lids
That melt the heart – a race apart – and we do as she gently bids.
How does she smile with tear filled eyes and melt a manly heart?
Just why does Dad go limp and weak *before* the crying starts?
Why can her arms twined round his neck ensure she has her way?
And she can use the same old tricks through each and everyday.
No matter what she does in life, she always has a charm,
Her knowledge came when she was born, and never means to harm,
She smooths the cat and strokes the dog and chats to next door's baby,
She knows her manners, beams her joys, like a little lady.
In just two years she's learnt to use the gifts that God has given
To please the man that's in her life from one till ninety-seven.
Her mum can recognise the ploy, but dad will never know
The 'Round The Finger Twisting' game, that through her life will flow.
Little girls all know of course, that males will always weaken,
But never will she let you know just where she learnt the lesson.

87

MAY 26TH
A serious consideration

OPPORTUNITY

If peace of mind came unasked or unearned to every single soul on earth, it would not be valued for the precious state of mind that it truly is, and the human race would be without that heaven sent opportunity to learn, and exercise the mind and soul towards true spiritual progression – there would be no real reason for earthly existence.

★　★　★

MAY 27TH
A smile with a moral

PUPPY LOVE

A puppy went out for a walk,
And stopped a wee mouse for a talk,
Said the mouse to the pup,
"Please tell me what's up
Ladies faces have gone white as chalk."

The puppy considered this fact,
And wondered just how he should act,
He was feeling quite sad
For this poor little lad
That a mouse could make ladies feel cracked!

So he picked up the friendly wee mouse,
Which he carried right back to his house,
He took it to 'Mum'
For her to have fun,
Was surprised when she started to grouse.

The puppy was puzzled by this,
It wasn't a state he would wish,
So the pup took compassion,
And started a fashion
Of giving the downtrodden a lift.

There's a moral of course to be found
From the thoughts of this nice little hound,
It matters not where,
Our kindness we share,
As long as our motive is sound!

PAVEMENT ARTIST

The poppy seed went flying by
  Tossed upon the wind,
Dipping low then twirling high,
  Trying to find a place to land.

A concrete slab was then espied,
  Snuggled against a wall,
And a craggy joint in which to hide,
  Where the poppy seed could fall.

The blessing of some sunny days,
  And goodly falls of rain
Splashing on this pathway,
  Brought the seed to life again.

There it grew with every shower
  In spite of all the odds,
A red and dainty wild flower,
  Scorned in garden flower beds.

The food was poor, the plant was small,
  But the poppy did its best,
It only grew four inches tall,
  And its brightness did the rest.

Many a passer-by was cheered,
  The joy you could not measure,
Because the winds of change had steered
  One seed to give such pleasure.

People too can cheer the world
  However modest be their deed,
Just like a poppy flower unfurled
  From a wild and lonely seed.

MAY 29TH
We need to search

SOME PEOPLE ARE THINKERS whilst others are Doers. Here and there we can find someone who does both.

89

MAY 30TH
Worth waiting for

WILD SUMMER FLOWERS

When cool winds bow to the month of May,
   Her own sweet perfume fills the air
To herald now a summer's day,
   With all that's beautiful and fair.

June brings forth the wild rose,
   Hiding her thorny stalk,
Like a charming lady in repose
   Belying her prickly talk.

The rosebay willow herb appears
   With sun warmed July days,
Tall and graciously she rears
   Her glorious head to heaven's gaze.

And then the vision quite supreme,
   The scarlet poppy to behold,
A woven carpet it would seem,
   Defiant, beautiful and bold.

We feast upon these wild sights,
   Embryos of our garden flowers,
Our souls are fed with these delights,
   And heaven's truth at last is ours.

MAY 31ST
Handle with care

EVERY END – A NEW BEGINNING

Every experience in life has its beginning, end, and the important part in the middle – the part we enjoy or hate, or something in between.

  Beginnings may occur with joy, optimism or dread. The ends we may welcome or wish they had not arrived. Either way, it is as well to remember that every end of one experience heralds another new one. If we welcome it calmly, with optimism, and with a determination to handle it with tender loving care, we will find the world a nicer place than we had perhaps previously thought.

90

JUNE

GNOME NONSENSE

JUNE

June's warm evening dips her head,
  In silent worship of the day.
The brightness of the day has fled,
  And blackbird sings his final lay.

The roses bare their hearts to God,
  And offer gifts of sweet perfume.
Proud peony heads begin to nod,
  And tiny daisies close each bloom.

June's evening shadows only lent,
  To cool the heat that follows May,
Enhances honeysuckle's scent,
  And teaches all the world to pray.

June gardens brightly come to life,
  Stagger the mind and feed the soul,
The colours blend and cast out strife,
  To point the way mankind should go.

★ ★ ★

JUNE 2ND
An explanation?

KARMA?

There is a peculiar fact of the human race, that a happy, law abiding family can produce a lone 'black sheep' – an unhappy soul determined to cause as much trouble as possible for both themselves and everybody else – in contradiction to the rest of the family. Such folk seem to bring trouble into the world with them, and these situations add considerable weight to the theories of Karma and Reincarnation. How else can such misfits be so adequately explained?

★ ★ ★

JUNE 3RD
A special thought

LOVE SHINES – beyond the bounds of mere earthly life and motive, it honours faith and trust in heavenly destiny.

Growing pains with a smile.

AN ORGANIC GARDENER'S PRAYER

If there's any gardening angels
    Looking for a job down here,
Please flap your wings in this direction,
    My garden's in a mess I fear.

For things are getting out of hand,
    I'm overrun with slugs,
Green fly on my roses dwell,
    And some other naughty bugs.

Moles are rising on the grass,
    The mice all eat my peas,
And though the birds sound very nice,
    They're eating all my seeds.

Outright war is not my game,
    And killing doesn't fit
Into my little plan of life,
    But they try my patience just a bit.

So I'd be very grateful
    If you could intervene,
And teach them better manners,
    Like the ladybirds I've seen.

But if you find their ears are deaf
    To the wisdom you have given,
Perhaps you'd bring a bus along,
    And drive them all to heaven!

JUNE 5TH
A thought for a cause.

SAVING TIME

What is the point of rushing through our daily tasks in order to save time, if at the end of the day we have found nothing worthwhile on which to use the time we have saved? If we paused for a few moments to reflect, we might find a very worthy cause for any spare time that we can create.

Pure humanity

A PAUSE FOR THOUGHT

In the daily bustle of our lives, it is so easy to take for granted the many wonders of our world, many of which we have already lost through ignorance or neglect.

Yet there are still countless miracles that touch our daily lives, which we can and must preserve – not only for ourselves and future generations – but in gratitude and compassion for all life on earth.

Who could hear a skylark singing with such powerful song, and watch it rising straight towards the sky without marvelling at the sheer strength and musical talent of such a tiny bird? How did Nature's hand design a coat of many colours for macaws, a tiny goldfinch, or the fantastic bird of paradise?

A pause to compare the cheetah with a man-made motor car, reveals that the cheetah can reach a speed of forty-five miles per hour in only two seconds – from a standing start – and quickly reach a speed of seventy miles per hour. We humans would be crawling by comparison.

Life on earth could not continue without the existence and rhythm of the sea, the moon and sun, the cleansing frost and winds, the rains that so often give us an excuse to complain.

If blackbirds and robins were no longer there to cheer the morning on, or daffodils no longer nodded golden heads with the rhythm of a gentle breeze, we would have a sad old world indeed. If summer flowers did not offer gifts of colour for our eyes and tease our noses with their perfume, it would be a dull old world indeed. How would we feel if these things were no longer there for us to see and hear – a silent spring, no colour in the flowers, no trees to shelter and give their strength and life to us and mother earth?

Yet for all the wonders and strength of nature, it is the human being – the people of the earth – us, who can preserve these wonders of the world or let them die away by our own selfishness and sheer stupidity.

When we think of all the help and comfort that mankind receives from the animal kingdom and the environment itself surely we should return the compliment in greater measure. The beauties and blessings of the world are many, it is for us to count them, pause for thought, and preserve them for all life, through conscience and pure humanity.

JUNE 7TH
Unnecessary pain

HAVE WE THE RIGHT?

All life that has a nervous system can feel pain, and when that pain is caused by animals in order to eat and survive in the wild, nature has provided methods of quick and easy dispatch for most of these situations. It is the Human Race that consistently causes unnecessary suffering and killing.

Wars, meat eating, acts of homicide, and thoughtless or uncaring attitudes in ordinary daily life, such as careless driving or the way pets, children and the elderly are sometimes treated, all can contribute to avoidable suffering and death. If we don't like the experience of pain ourselves, have we any right to allow it for other life on earth? Some people seem to think we have, whilst others condemn it yet do little to reduce it. Perhaps we could all do a little more to reduce the suffering and so give ourselves the right to have some pride in the reduction of pain.

JUNE 8TH
A thought in the garden

SUMMER BOUQUET

The warming sun of golden days
  To coax a rose-bud to full bloom,
To see a butterfly that plays,
  Intoxicated with perfume.

Delphinium raises saintly head,
  Competing with the sky so blue,
Towering over the pansy bed,
  To show what honey-bees can do.

Marguerites are standing there,
  Trying to imitate the sun,
With orange centred heart to share
  Her petalled rays with everyone.

Among the flowers the gardener toils,
  Enhancing nature's fine display,
His guiding hand with hoe and soils
  Creating summer's grand bouquet.

96

JUNE 9TH
An unlikely power

THE WORLD OF FRIENDSHIP

Friendships can be a curious mix, we usually think of them as a partnership between people – mainly folk of like minds, although opposites can also blend in friendships. But they can also occur between animals and people or link two animals. Unlikely friendships can arise between two animals that would normally be considered adversaries – dogs and cats are well known examples. Cats and pets birds or even a mouse or rabbit are not unknown partnerships. These reflections help to demonstrate the value, extent and strength of friendships – however extraordinary it may seem. We are reminded by such animals that people have a lot to learn from both them and the world of friendship.

JUNE 10TH
A giggle rhyme

GNOME NONSENSE

I'm not quite sure what I should do
To prompt a smile or a giggle or two.
I know! I've got a good idea,
For I usually find a Funny to cheer,
I'll sit myself in a flower pot,
Pretend I'm a blue Forget-Me-Not.
Remember me when life's a tangle,
You've gotta laugh, find a funny angle.
The simplest things will do the trick
To clear the doldrums nice and quick,
So when there's too much gloom about,
Jump in a flower pot and shout!
This cockeyed plan will make your day –
Drive all those horrid blues away.
Hooray for little giggle rhymes,
They'll see you through to better times!

97

"ALL THE WORLD'S A STAGE"

The nightingale sings his lonely aria –
  The operatic star of woods and trees,
People are directors and the stagehands
  In theatres of wild places such as these.

Thus we capture many magic moments
  Of sights and sounds of nature's natural stage.
We must never let there be a final curtain,
  But preserve the magic for a future age.

The stage of life has every kind of talent
  Passing through its special own stage door,
Some are stars by every kind of testing,
  Some are simply there to sweep the floor.

It matters not the way of human casting,
  For every single soul can play a part,
A few will be the nightingales of living,
  For most the task of life will be support.

But in the final time of life's assessment,
  The size of role we play is not the guide,
The *way* we've played the part that we've been given,
  Is the measure that will help our God decide.

DRIFTWOOD

Drifting thoughts can make or break our days, depending on the way we let them drift. We only need to watch a piece of driftwood tossing to and fro upon the sea in every direction, maybe washing on to a sandy beach or rocky outcrop, or shuttled out to sea again on an ebbing tide – to realise its relationship with our own thinking. The flotsam and jetsam of human thinking can land safety on the seashore of life towards productive action, or so easily drift upon the seas of waste and insignificance, eventually to rot away for lack of caring and someone's rescuing hand. That someone has the insight to recognise a worthy use for a piece of driftwood of our coastline sea, or a drifting thought on the sea of life.

A CHANCE TO LEARN

If no-one ever suffered,
　And there was never any pain,
No-one could use compassion
　To restore good health again.

If no-one had the chance to give
　Compassion's helping hand,
No-one could find the path to God,
　Or answer His command.

If no-one ever suffered,
　There'd be no chance to learn
To give and take with equal grace,
　Or feel a real concern.

If no-one ever saw despair
　In pleading canine eyes,
Or watched a helpless feline's look,
　We'd never hear their anguished cries.

If no-one ever felt the pain
　Of seeing someone suffer,
We'd never know the healing love
　That we can share with one another.

The blessings of this world are found
　By contrast to the pain,
How else would people know the truth
　That sunshine follows rain?

We need progression for the soul,
　To raise compassion's healing sights,
The pain and suffering of this world
　Helps us reach those greater heights.

★ ★ ★

COURAGE

The bright light of courage and bravery shines like a brilliant star on the darkness of despair.

A worthy gift

SACRIFICE

From birth to our final days on earth, we are called upon to make sacrifices to help others. It is the way we deal with these situations that sorts the loving from the uncaring, the kind from the unkind, the evolved soul from the unthinking one. It is a special form of giving, and much depends on whether we give graciously or reluctantly. Our own conscience can tell us into which category we fall – if we have the courage to listen.

The personal sacrifices that we make for others, clearly have nothing in common with the ceremonial blood sacrifice of animals, or even human beings, so beloved of many religious doctrines through the ages. It was, and occasionally still is, a practice that hurts both perpetrator and the victim that had no choice but to be slain at the will of a human being. Even if motive is designed to look right, conscience is still available to sort the right from wrong. Sacrifice must help another, not destroy it, if the sacrifice is to be worthwhile. It can only be worthwhile when it is a personal gift to another life, for in that way it is a gift to God.

★ ★ ★

JUNE 16TH
Nonsense with reasoning

YOUNG PONDERINGS

As I'm only five years old,
    I'd think it very funny
If I'd got only arms and legs,
    But hadn't got a tummy.

But if I had no food to eat,
    And hadn't any money,
I'd think that I was lucky,
    That I *hadn't* got a tummy.

'Cos lots of little boys and girls
    With tummies grown quite big,
Have no food to fill them up,
    They'll be hungry I would think.

I'm glad that I have all the things
    That make me very happy,
I *must* ask God to tell grown-ups
    To make those other children comfy.

100

THE WILD ROSE

How could the wild rose have known
    Its wondrous contribution
With grafted cuttings, seeds well sown,
    And world-wide distribution.

So perfect are our garden flowers
    In colour, form and grace,
Rounded bushes, hanging bowers,
    From the wild rose we trace.

The nurtured progress of the rose
    And the evolution of mere man,
Side by side the challenge grows
    Since gardening began.

If man could just improve himself
    As he has enhanced the rose,
The world at last would find itself
    Steeped in sweet repose.

Yet we must not forget the source
    Of our lovely garden rose,
Her wild cousin reigns supreme,
    In majestic country hedgerows.

SILENCE IS GOLDEN No. 6

True silence is beautiful, but too much of it and it would lose its value for us, indeed we would probably tire of it, even resent it. It is because of its contrast with our noisy daily lives that it becomes a magical experience, and the harder it is to find, the more we value it – rare diamonds of the soul, so beautiful that earthly eyes cannot comprehend them – the silent music of the mind that makes some silent moments golden and divine.

DAWN MIDST THE HILLS AND VALLEYS

The eastern morning star is fading
　As the sun comes o'er the hill,
The sloping meadows now are bending,
　With morning's undulating skill
To tell of gentle dips and rising,
　Which only sunrise can reveal.

Streaks of light across the river,
　Reflection from the sturdy shore,
Turns darkness into shining silver
　To lift all lonely hearts once more,
For sunrise is the great redeemer
　Of cherished hopes and nature's law.

The message of the hills and valleys
　Brought to life by morning sun,
Fading out the dips and worries,
　Renewing hope for everyone,
Happiness the song it carries,
　Echoing the joys to come.

Now the morning star has faded,
　The sun is high above the hills,
All the dips the morn paraded
　Level out as blackbird trills,
The magic of this dawn is cradled
　In the arms of nature's will.

TRY, TRY, TRY AGAIN

No one need despair if they fail to reach a high ideal, it may not have been a suitable one for them in the first place, but if it is right, then some positive thinking, determination and a prayer, can between them, work a miracle.

TRUE LOVE

True unadulterated love could solve the problems of Mankind and all the world.
We have to learn to give it.

★ ★ ★

JUNE 22ND
Fair play with a smile

ANYONE FOR TENNIS?

Why is it that tennis balls
   Have a bouncing will of their own?
No matter how you cut and slice
   Some balls it has been known –
Will bounce in odd directions
   Where your point just can't be won!

Life too is like a tennis ball,
   Not bouncing as it ought,
No matter how we play our shots,
   Some balls go out of court,
But we can learn to play the game
   The way the Master taught.

Sometimes we find the score is deuce,
   And it's hard to win the game,
Advantage seems to come and go
   And your opponent feels the same,
But every point must be fairly won
   Without rancour, fear or shame.

But tennis balls are kindly too,
   To skim the net, or fall
Just inside the tramlines –
   And make it thirty all!
Or drop inside the baseline
   With a spin that's a winning call!

Our daily lives can serve an ace
   As we send that winning ball
Across the challenging net of time,
   Standing straight and tall,
Playing in an honest cause
   To win game and set, and final call.

JUNE 23RD
Granny's wisdom

A PLACE FOR EVERYTHING –

AND EVERYTHING IN ITS PLACE – a saying from grandmother's time, that was designed to encourage the younger generation to put their toys and clothes away and so avoid a muddled existence. These words were actually wisdom of much greater significance than Granny ever envisaged, for it isn't just a case of tidiness, most things of earthly life do better in their own natural environment – everything in its place.

Tramps are not happy in palaces, and kings and queens would not be happy living as tramps. Primroses prefer woodlands, roses like sunshine, once we move them from their natural habitat, like all flowers they need coaxing and protection.

It happens in the animal world as well. Polar bears are designed for cold wild places, not the warm confines of a zoo. Budgerigars and parrots should be flying free in a naturally warm climate – if we move them to cages and human living rooms, we have to take special care to prevent illness and neurosis because they are out of their natural environment. This principle can be observed in almost any sphere of earthly life. Perhaps it applies to the human race as well. Maybe the people of the world would be happier where they are born, they may be designed for that environment – its climate, food, work and living conditions. At least it would save a lot of effort to make changes to suit people who move around the world into different conditions to their own, for everyone would be in their right place, the one designed for them in the first place.

There are many far apart places where climatic conditions are nevertheless similar, but closer inspection will reveal many differences in vegetation, terrain and culture, and these are problems that have to be accommodated or overcome. Perhaps they are a challenge to the adventurer, who traditionally rarely counts the cost of his adventures. Or perhaps the adventurer's place *is* world-wide, just another demonstration of everyone and everything being in the right place, at the right time.

JUNE 24TH
Priceless

A FRIEND can be the most precious gift on earth, yet it is something that money can't buy.

104

NIGHT-TIME

Night clouds slide away o'er distant hills,
To carry sleep and rest to foreign parts
As waking minds compete with sleepy wills,
Reluctant eyes and such half-hearted hearts
That yet we wonder how a day fulfils
The needs and tasks before next night-time starts.

But evening shadows drift back home once more,
Ending yet another glorious day
As they left that distant foreign shore
While we have worked and played our time away.
The wonder of the evening creates its great encore,
The night clouds bring us peace again, and another chance to pray.

Our night-time sleep renews our strength and courage,
Mending aching limbs and hearts alike,
As guardians of our souls give us the privilege
Of tending us with loving dreams of light.
How foolish we who dare not steer the carriage
That bears the many blessings of the night.

For what reason do we fear the night-time shadows
When we know they're part of God's own perfect plan?
For even if we haven't earned our halos,
We've surely done the very best we can.
So let us greet the joys of our tomorrows
Through the blessings of the night-time gift to man.

JUNE 26TH
Not a very good reason

IT COULD MEAN SO MUCH

It does seem a pity that people sometimes refrain from offering help in case they are thought to be interfering. It seems that we have to be in a really desperate situation before many people feel it is safe to offer help – a sad reflection on human relationships, especially when we realise it is only fear that delays or prevents help that could mean so much to someone.

TWO LITTLE LADYBIRDS

Two little ladybirds were sitting on a rose,
What they were doing there, goodness only knows,
But when they had finished it, their spots were all aglow
And a thousand baby ladybirds were on their way to show –
Why two little ladybirds never can say "No!"

So when the ladybirds have lived their little lives right through,
They'll carry on, their service give, just like me and you.
They'll fly away to heaven of course, and join the other few
Who left a legacy of spots to find a rose or two,
For without these happy ladybirds, what would our roses do?

★ ★ ★

THE GIFT OF WATER

Water – the lifeblood of the world, from trickling stream to mighty ocean and one of our most essential assets. We love it or grumble about it depending on it being the right amount and whether or not it comes at the right time and in the right place.

All animal life also depends on water in some way or other, many have already died or suffered severely from lack of it, or even too much of it in the wrong place. We treat it carelessly at our peril, for some parts of the world have already been turned into desert because of Mankind's foolishness and his mismanagement. We have the knowledge to restore the balance, but have we the will to use that knowledge? Those who understand are too often a cry in the wilderness of humanity, those who could, tend to turn a deaf ear because of the cost, forgetting that money will be of no use in a desert!

Modern technology about irrigation systems, conserving water, and returning vast areas to their previous natural states with tree and vegetation planting would certainly be a costly project that would require much goodwill and international co-operation, but it could be done and would demonstrate out true appreciation of the gift of water.

JUNE 29TH
Undying love

WARM WELCOME

In earthly terms death implies an end in its entirety, with nothing in the future. It is an earthly word, that we use to describe the transition between earthly existence and heavenly life. Life itself is indestructible and can only change in form as we know it for earthly conditions. Transition to a wider existence, is in fact a freedom we cannot comprehend in earthly terms.

All religions teach survival after earthly death, only in the detail of earthly thinking do they vary in their concept of life. The weakness of most of them is that they rely on faith alone without proof of their theories, and human faith can be so frail. Yet there is a way to allow our loved ones in Spirit (not dead or sleeping, or dwelling in some far off land of human imagination) to come to us and prove their own survival and their continued love and help towards us. The simplicity of opening hearts and minds to the awareness of their presence, opens the door for them to visit us, be with us and help us whenever we may need the help they offer. We may not see them, yet we might. We cannot touch them as we once did, but they have the power and knowledge to touch us – if we will allow them to do so, just a feather touch or a soft breeze away, perhaps with a scent or perfume we can recognise, perhaps a sound that is familiar. These are expressions of love and affection, and who would really dare to suggest that such sincerity and love can be wrong?

Real love and kindness is right according to any true religious teaching. It is for those of us who still live within the confines of earthly existence, to welcome those we love, just as we have always done.

JUNE 30TH
Round the corner?

HOPE

Forgive the world its harsh reality,
Its lack of hospitality,
For there is hope around you still,
Your dearest dream can yet fulfil.
For there's new kindness everyday,
Some of it will come your way,
There's understanding flowing free,
For those who have the eyes to see.

107

JULY

THE THOUGHTS OF FLORA EXOTICA

JULY

Perfume wafting on the breeze,
   Warm yet fresh with morning dew,
A rising prayer up to the trees,
   There for all, but known to few.

Sweet pea and mignonette are there,
   To scent the air that's angel sent,
Roses, stocks will add their share,
   Remember well, it's only lent.

Delphiniums rise in majesty,
   Reflect the sky with sundry blues,
Delight the eyes of those that see
   The heaven there within those blooms.

Poppies wave in moving air,
   Petals fine as butterflies.
Exotic blossoms fine and rare,
   And hollyhocks that reach the skies.

Early fruits come abundantly,
   To those who worked to give them life,
Rewards that come eternally,
   With July garden's pure delight.

★ ★ ★

JULY 2ND
Time well spent

A PAUSE TO LEARN

If we pause to learn from the uplifting moments of life or advents of success, rather than just take such experiences for granted, their value is doubled to us by learning from them as well as taking the pleasure or happiness they offer, which has to be time well spent.

IF THEY COULD TALK

If the animals could talk to us,
 I wonder what they'd say
About the things we do to them
 In our unthinking way.

When a lamb is led to slaughter,
 Would it make a last appeal?
Would a fox that's being hunted,
 Request a final meal?

Maybe baby seals would beg
 A stay of execution,
Perhaps a dolphin then would ask
 That we stop the sea's pollution.

A chicken in her battery cage
 Would surely beg release,
So that she might spread her wings,
 And scratch about in peace.

A rabbit trapped for all its life
 In an experimental cage,
Would surely squeal its own appeal,
 In its fear and pain and rage.

If only they could talk to us
 About these dreadful things –
But it's a case of pigs might fly
 If only they had wings!

But of course we should not need
 The animals to say,
That they feel pain just as we do,
 All through each passing day.

But if we lent a listening ear
 Through the conscience of mankind,
We'd hear the plea of the animals
 For a kinder state of mind.

If the animals could talk to us
 Their thanks they'd offer too,
For all the help of kinder folk,
 And the things they try to do.

112

GRANNY'S PRAYER

I held the baby in my arms,
  So small, so beautiful and happy,
With gurgling smile she touched my heart,
  For her years ahead are many.

I pray her ups and downs in life
  Teach heaven's wisdom to this child,
That she may learn true happiness,
  And her soul be undefiled.

May this baby learn compassion
  With each advancing year,
And receive the same from other folk,
  To cast out want and fear.

Please may her lessons be not harsh
  As she wends her way through time,
And may another baby smile
  Make her ageing life sublime.

May blessings follow you each day
  And darker days be few,
All these and every happiness
  Are your Granny's prayer for you.

JULY 5TH
Dislocated ears?

THE TRUTH OF THE MATTER

There are times when honesty becomes a matter of opinion, rather than the spiritual level of thought it actually is. Even the voice of conscience can be heard incorrectly – if we do not wish to hear aright.

A GOOD SAMARITAN

Two little blue tits were arguing
About which nut to take,
All of them looked tempting,
The choice was hard to make.

They didn't even notice
A hawk was flying by,
Whose attention was diverted,
By a kindly butterfly.

The many flutters of her wings
Upset hawky concentration,
And enabled our two little tits
To avoid a confrontation!

People too can do good turns
To help a soul less wise,
Who fail to see a danger near,
And so need butterflies.

★ ★ ★

JULY 7TH
The hiding place

THE HOME OF HAPPINESS

So many people mistake pleasure for happiness. True inner happiness is a contentment of the soul and must be earned by service, whilst pleasure can be bought and sold or sought in the wrong places and is generally an experience of the material world. Pleasure is not wrong if it is given and accepted in an unselfish way and for the right motive, yet pleasure is but a shadow of the true happiness which dwells within the soul to give and receive, share perfection and the dreams of hope with all humanity.

FRIENDS AND RELATIONS

We are given our relations, but we choose our friends. It is up to each of us to choose aright, but it is worth remembering that our relations can also be our friends, and very often are.

★ ★ ★

NATURE'S EVENSONG

The music of the evening sings a gentle lullaby,
As blackbird trills his final song before he says goodbye
To every daytime stress and joy, its passing hopes and fears,
Appearing to be new and yet, the same through passing years.

The final twitter in the hedge as the sparrows say good-night,
And catch the tired mood of evening, with its gently fading light,
While crickets chirrup merrily as they're rising from their beds,
Along with owls that blink to life, to hoot and turn their heads.

A distant fox will bark his call in quiet woodland dell,
And vixen shriek her welcome note to say that all is well.
A flying bat will squeak in flight as on its way it goes
To catch its supper on the wing, as the glow-worm brightly glows.

A cracking twig and croaking frog add rhythm to the air,
A rustle in the undergrowth, from we know not where.
The rippling stream flows on and on, tumbling over stones,
The fir trees sway in rhythm too, tossing down their cones.

The poplars whisper in the wind the secret they must tell
That moon and stars are shining in the heavens where they dwell.
The peaceful ending of the day, which seemed so loud and long,
Is purified and given rest, with nature's evensong.

JULY 10TH
Full circle

MESSAGES FROM THE FLOWERS

Tulip time is springtime, a time of new hopes and strength, with a whisper of warmer summer days to come. The primroses and daffodils have already completed their task of heralding that outburst of new life and young leaf buds that turn the brown of winter into glorious shades of green.

We next survey blue carpets of memory in the dainty appeal of forget-me-nots, as they charm the soil beneath the roses that will soon be in full bloom, to gladden the eye and satisfy perceptive human noses.

Roses may be designed by gardeners and horticultural scientists into every colour, style and size, but each one's history is the wild rose of the hedgerow, which charms us still, and calls the bees to work and hum their summer song.

When that first flush of roses begins to slip away along with tall delphiniums and smaller annual flowers, we know that autumn will soon be coming into sight with mature leaves of golden hues, only the simple daisy flower will remain to remind us of the endurance of simplicity.

And then at last, we notice bright red berries on our shrubs, probably we did not even notice they earlier had flowers, and this reminds us that the full potential of many people, as well as flowers and shrubs, occurs later in their lives, later in the year or years according to their kind and task in life, and all will respond to tender loving care.

At the end of every flowering year, when all seems lost and dark, we can still find the shy Christmas rose. Winter Jasmine shining brightly in her golden mantle, and here and there an early primrose tells us that life is not dead but sleeping, and soon will rise again with all the flowers of spring, a message of hope and encouragement to people who may be negotiating a dark patch in their own lives, reminding them that all life has its cycle of light and dark, so that they can look towards the bright display of life and flowers that is certainly on its way. The flowers can give us so many messages, it is for us to listen – and the wiser souls will learn from the mystery and quiet secrets that they bring.

★ ★ ★

JULY 11TH
A puzzle!

THE QUESTION. Why is it that so many animal lovers eat meat?

116

JULY 12TH
Tact!

DRY TOAST

Honest words, advice and opinions can be very helpful, but there are times when they can be unappetizing – like dry toast. A little tact – like butter and jam can make an enormous difference to the taste.

★ ★ ★

JULY 13TH
Wise nonsense

BUZZ

I'm a happy bumblebee,
Busy as heck as you can see.
I'm getting ready with my pen,
Buzzing to work but can't say when.
I'm hoping now to write a letter,
But reckon you could do much better.
I'd bumble all the words along,
So I'll buzz my message in a song,
And hum a very special tune,
I'm sure you'll get the message soon
That I'm not very good at writing,
My work with flowers is more exciting.
There my efforts aren't in vain,
And you my friend can do the same.
Just use the gifts that you have got,
You'll lift a sad world quite a lot!

★ ★ ★

JULY 14TH
Some second thoughts are best

THOUGHTLESSNESS

With clumsy knowledge and lack of proper thought, it is so easy to spoil the beautiful moments of our lives, and so easy to spoil such rare and special moments for others.

117

IF ONLY –

If only I had known,
  I would have done much better,
If I'd known then, what I know now,
  I'd have followed to the letter.
If only I had realised
  The situation at the time,
I could have used a different plan
  To the one I thought was mine.

And yet I can't help wondering,
  Why things happen as they do,
The picture never is complete,
  The clues are far too few.
And yet there *is* a pattern,
  A guiding hand and voice,
To all life's sundry problems
  To help us make a choice.

So maybe things are meant to be
  A little bit uncertain,
Or else we'd never have the chance
  To use our intuition.
Perhaps God in His wisdom,
  Meant life to be this way,
Maybe we shouldn't question
  His plans for us each day.

If only we could think like Him,
  And know the master plan,
We'd have a better chance perhaps,
  To do the best we can.
And yet I think it safer,
  That we *don't* know everything,
We'd make a frightful muddle
  If *our* plans came into being.

If only I could realise,
  That God can guide our lives,
I'd learn to follow faithfully –
  If only I were wise.
If only we were wise enough
  We could make a better choice,
Many problems wouldn't happen
  If we heard that guiding voice.

A PLACE IN THE WILD

In the wild places of the world,
  Nature's lonely secrets hide and dwell,
From mountain top to arid plain below,
  And churning sea to quiet forest dell.

No man should ever spoil the quiet haven,
  Where lizard pokes his ever nervous head,
Or deer be startled from their silent browsing,
  Nor hedgehog turfed from leafy winter bed.

The buzzard flies the wild and windy moorland,
  The dolphin plays and leaps around the seas,
While polar bear will guard his icy homestead,
  The koala nibbles eucalyptus leaves.

All the wild places of the world,
  Are needed by the fauna that is free,
Man takes this land for over-population,
  The folly of his greed he cannot see.

Let curlews cry the plea for isolation,
  Let nature keep some places undefiled,
May the finer side of man respond with greatness,
  And guard the secret places of the wild.

JULY 17TH
An open door

A REASON FOR SUFFERING

Ours is not to reason why,
Ours to only weep and cry,
But tears can cleanse a lonely soul
Help a life to reach its goal,
For suffering teaches understanding,
And paves the path to gracious living.
Our patience and sincerity,
Opens the door of spirituality.

JULY 18TH
Silent beauty

SILENCE IS GOLDEN No. 7

The peace of a woodland dell, with the silent beauty of wild flowers and soundless flutter of butterfly wings, these are a silence to cherish.

JULY 19TH
Universal love

A THOUGHT FOR THE FUTURE

May the conscience of mankind,
  Be expressed in caring love,
To ever seek for truth and find
  The peaceful message of the dove
To dwell in every heart and mind,
  Its honesty to prove.

May the peoples of the earth
  Learn peace within their hearts,
And find a spiritual rebirth
  As all evil thought departs,
That man may know the silent worth
  Universal love imparts.

May the sanctity of Spirit
  Filter into every troubled mind,
That love may prove its gentle merit,
  And anxious hearts may find
The love that has no limit,
  In the world that God designed.

JULY 20TH
Towards tolerance

A MOTE OF NOTE

No-one is perfect, and the mote in our own eye can help us understand the weaknesses of others. The tolerance that this teaches can be a basis of true friendships.

120

JULY 21ST
A flowering snob?
(with a smile)

THE THOUGHTS OF FLORA EXOTICA

I know that I am beautiful,
    I have dignity and grace,
These other flowers are quite small,
    With a less exotic face.

All the gardeners love me,
    I'm a symbol of their skill,
I'm protected from the slugs and things,
    Which my gardening friends will kill.

I'm watched over very carefully,
    Unlike those daisies there
That ornament the nice green lawn,
    And make the gardener tear his hair.

Those dandelions – yellow bright,
    Look just like small chrysanths,
But try to tell a gardener that,
    And he won't offer thanks!

I haven't any perfume now,
    And that I do regret,
It's all been lost in breeding,
    But I'd love to have it back!

It's just the simple flowers,
    Like violets and thyme
That put my nose quite out of joint,
    And make me feel less fine.

So when you gaze on me with pride,
    Fulfilling a gardener's need,
Remember that ere the gardener came to life,
    I too was a humble weed!

JULY 22ND
An odd question

HOW CAN THIS BE?

How can it be that there are so many people needing help, so many animals needing care, and so many wild places needing protection, and so many people that are bored to tears because they have nothing important to do?

121

JULY 23RD
Negative V positive

THE WORRY FACTOR

Worrying by itself is aimless, disorganised thinking that solves nothing, achieves nothing but can easily cause us to be ill. It can become a bad habit that it is hard to break, but it can be done.

Worriers are usually people who care about a great many things – situations, people, animals, the environment, trees and plants, almost anything in fact. Caring can be a very positive attitude to benefit all these aspects of life, and so, in turn the carer.

Negative worrying is such a waste of time and good intention, whilst caring in a positive way is the channelling of worrying thoughts into useful action. That action may need physical application, or perhaps a prayer or healing thought. In one or other of these ways we can all do something to help improve a bad or negative situation. The secret is to sit quietly and sort our worries into the different categories that we can accomplish, and then simply do them. We will find ourselves too busy to waste our time on worry for its own sake.

Caring people can often prevent an undesirable occurrence, or even a disaster, simply because their in-built sensitivity alerts them to hidden dangers. It is not a particularly easy existence, but a very useful and rewarding one if this sensitivity and caring attitude is channelled in a right and positive way. It can then be a gift of the spirit worthy of the title.

JULY 24TH
A morning purpose

THE DAY BEGINS

Still as the night-time,
Yet in the morning light
Nothing stirs, except the birds
That know the time is right
For man to rise above the sloth of inactivity,
And do his best with daytime creativity,
And bear in mind his duty to his fellow man,
Furthering the purpose of God's eternal plan,
That all life on earth may share such bounty,
In kindness, peace and loving generosity.

122

A song of the sea

SEAGULLS

With long and graceful wings swept wide
    She challenges the ocean,
Gliding, diving, rising yet again,
    Demonstrating perfect flight in motion.

She catches daily sustenance at sea,
    Or takes a crafty chance upon the shore –
Cadging someone's half devoured sandwich,
    Or following the farmer's plough for more.

She shrieks her call from any seaside housetop,
    Or blends her song with rhythmic crashing waves,
As stormy winds provide the background music,
    Her cry will pierce the cacophony of staves.

She tucks her nest on some protruding outcrop,
    Where we would think her babies were unsafe,
But in her wisdom she provides the guardian,
    With overhanging rocks and steep cliff face.

The magic of the seabirds never fails us,
    Such tiny strength that braves an angry sea,
A lesson from the seagulls to us humans,
    To cultivate the courage to be free.

Yet their quarrels imitate us foolish humans,
    With noisy argument, and thoughtless greedy ways,
But here again they demonstrate their purpose,
    To survive the rough and tumble of their days.

But we who also know the purpose,
    Of living here on earth for just awhile,
Still can survive, yet with the kinder knowledge
    Towards the universal love that God provides.

So let us love and cheer the graceful seagull,
    Admire her skill, forgive her noisy ways,
For we must share the sea and lifetime with her,
    Perhaps her cry is just a song of praise.

★ ★ ★

JULY 26TH
Step by step

THE BLESSINGS of real happiness come with true friendships.
The blessings of true friendships come with unselfish thinking.

Avoidable suffering

PAIN

We have all known it at some time in our lives, from as far back as babyhood. Nobody likes it, some will bravely suffer it in a good cause. Most people fear it and many have to tolerate it in illness or accident, but sometimes it is the result of deliberate action or thoughtlessness by someone else. Animals in particular are victims of this cause of pain, who rarely bring it on themselves as is often the case with human pain.

The phases of avoidable animal pain vary from the careless or thoughtless action of a pet owner to deliberate infliction for human gain or gratification. Many people profit financially from the killing or torture of animals, while others inflict the pain as part of sports and pastimes. Countless numbers of people allow it in the name of food. Most people pay lip service to an abhorrence of deliberately inflicted pain, and most of these do little to end or reduce it. Here and there a voice is raised in defence of the animal kingdom and the voices are increasing as more and more people become aware that pain is universal. As the voices of compassion become louder, there is no excuse for the rest of humanity to fail to hear the appeal and the cry of the animals. Their pain can so easily be ours.

JULY 28TH
A growing courage

A GARDEN OF HEALING

Courage shines like a million stars
　In the galaxy of life,
To heal the sick and cover the scars
　Of pain, old sorrow and strife.

And you my friend may know the power
　Of a healing angel's hand,
For courage guides that spirit flower
　To the garden of your mind.

There it can grow in fine array,
　With the strength your tending gives,
A new bud blossoms everyday,
　For courage is the flower that lives.

124

Thoughts about bees

THE MIRACLE OF THE BEES

Not long ago, trees were pink
   With blossom on the boughs,
Like cotton wool or candy floss,
   Charmed into a billion flowers.

The bees arrived to play their part
   According to natures plan,
To gild the trees with luscious fruit
   As sustenance for man.

This mystery of life on earth,
   That man can so depend
On tiny bees to give him food,
   Is a miracle without end.

JULY 30TH
Beauty in the rain

WELCOME the glory of summer flowers, but remember their need of spring time showers!

★ ★ ★

JULY 31ST
An accidental smile

THE VISITOR

A little mouse popped in to see
What we'd got for him for tea.
Cheese was "Off" and cake crumbs too,
What's a poor wee mouse to do?
There's other things to find of course,
Soap and candles, Worcester sauce.
But none of these have much appeal
If something nicer he can steal.
But stealing isn't mousy game,
Harsh hunger is the cause of blame.
I'll accidentally drop some meat
My pussy has declined to eat.
I wouldn't like to be a mouse,
In a cold, unfriendly, foodless house!

AUGUST

SAFE JOURNEYS

AUGUST 1ST
Summer stardom

AUGUST

The brilliant warmth of an August day,
Nostalgic scent of new mown hay,
A mass of flowers in fine array,
To teach us mortals how to pray,
And bless the month of August.

And so Man's ills receive some pardon,
Through the joy of an August garden,
As colours scramble in profusion
In every corner, quite unbidden,
To bless the August stardom.

AUGUST 2ND
In tune with the world

THE RHYTHMS OF LIFE

The rhythm of life is not one long monotonous drumming of time as some people would have us believe. The rhythms of life change with passing months or years or different situations. It is for us to listen and be in tune with life, adjusting our timing and rhythm to whatever situation we find ourselves dealing with. Then the notes will not jar our ears, and we will no longer find ourselves out of time and tune with our surroundings and perhaps the rest of the world.

★ ★ ★

AUGUST 3RD
Lightening the load

HAPPINESS IS FOR SHARING, and those who share this gift with others, find they have earned the right to share their sorrows too, and so lighten their own load at a less happy time of their lives.

129

LADYBIRDS

Have you ever wondered why
The ladybird has spots?
The brilliant armoury she wears
All spotted with black dots?

A warning sign for all to see,
That she would taste quite bitter,
That she is sour and not quite nice
As anybody's dinner!

If people too would carry flags,
To warn of sour minds,
The rest of us could turn away
When we see the signs.

Perhaps they do and we don't see
As often as we should,
The spotted human ladybird,
But if we tried – we could!

But let us not forget the good
A ladybird can do,
And human ladybirds the same,
They have their good points too!

AUGUST 5TH
To lighten our darkness

KINDNESS has so many faces,
Dwells in many secret places.
KINDNESS heals when all else fails,
Lends a strength when courage quails.
KINDNESS gives without return,
A shining truth that all may learn.
KINDNESS brings a shining light
To illuminate the darkest night.

MORNING ARTISTRY

Have you ever watched a sunrise
    Peeping over distant hills?
Have you ever seen the magic
    That wispy clouds reveal
As they create pure artistry,
    Our hearts and minds to fill?

Have you witnessed sunrise colour
    Of fiery red and brilliant gold?
Reflecting on the autumn leaves
    With such beauty growing old?
Have you ever heard the silence
    That early morning can unfold?

If you have found this silent beauty
    In the secret hours of dawn,
And felt the tears of gratitude
    Brought forth by such a morn –
You are at one with nature's plan
    Since the day that you were born.

If only every soul could know
    This wonder of the sun,
Its early morning artistry
    That's free for everyone,
Then all could feel the peace of mind
    That the dawning has become.

MIRACLES

Miracles don't just happen. Someone sees a need, plans and organises the necessary action, and that someone will be on the Other Side of life – some may call it Heaven. There will be a team of helpers and some of those will be living on Our Side of life, people who are willing to be used, either consciously or unconsciously – in the manufacture of a miracle.

AUGUST 8TH
Quiet courage

A SPECIAL KIND OF LOVE

When patient love is tested
  Every moment of each day,
The angels will protect you
  As you walk your chosen way.

When a kindly smile is rising
  Over all adversity,
It sets a fine example
  For a naughty world to see.

When your gentle help is given
  As part of daily bread,
It feeds the souls of other folk
  Who can't see the way ahead.

When understanding of another soul
  Reveals an angelic mind,
Then quiet courage walks with you
  Through the problems that you find.

But when your mercy task is done
  And tears and pain retreat,
The angels bring their own reward,
  With happiness complete.

Thus the tests of life and time
  Have built a saintly soul,
That knows the joy of service given
  With unselfish love and toil.

AUGUST 9TH
A natural gift

OUR INSTINCT can be a wonderful guide to a right course of action. We are born with this gift of self-preservation, and animals use it effectively all the time. The human race could lose it through sheer lack of use, and denial of its existence.

132

AUGUST 10TH
Young wisdom

A FREE GIFT IN THE SHOPPING CENTRE

There was a lot of clatter and noise in the Shopping Centre. The weekend shoppers jostled for space as they anxiously pushed their way around, trying to find this and that, some wondering if they could afford the items anyway, some hurrying to get away whilst others caused a traffic jam as they gossiped to a friend they'd met, about a third party who it seemed didn't know the proper way to do something or other. Two people argued loudly so that other folk could hear their difference of opinion, while shopkeepers looked anxiously on, wishing people would come and buy instead of just talking or rushing about.

Suddenly an excited shriek cut through the bedlam of noise and confusion, a boy of four to five years was tugging on his mother's arm outside a flower shop. "Mum" he shouted, "Can I take some of those home to my Nan?" His mother hesitated a moment before stepping back towards the shop window. The background clatter had suddenly subsided as she pointed to different flowers in the window in consultation with her son, before they quietly disappeared into the shop, as the hubbub of the crowd drifted to a halt.

For a few brief moments, a little child had stilled the cacophony of noise and unthinking battle with time. He had produced a loving thought from the confusion of noise, unkind words and senseless bustle of adults all around him. Such is the wisdom of a child.

AUGUST 11TH
God's garden

HEALING WORDS

The blessing of a healing word,
Is Spirit's healing power.
When words of peace and love are heard,
The healing is in flower.

When healing words flow rich and free
To take away all gloom,
They gather so that all may see
God's garden in full bloom.

133

AUGUST 12TH
Baby knowledge?

A HIDDEN MEMORY?

The baby was desperately trying to avoid the tinned baby food which was labelled Beef. His mother explained between the baby yells of protest, that she had this problem everyday, and he wouldn't stop until they got to the pudding. Can it be that some children are being born into this world with a natural abhorrence to meat? There are it seems, quite a lot of children exhibiting a revulsion to it, without any actual knowledge of its origin. How could they have such knowledge unless they brought it into the world with them? – perhaps as a result of experience in a previous earthly life?

AUGUST 13TH
A plodding smile

SAFE JOURNEYS

I may be slow, but I'll have you know
  That I get there in the end,
And people too, should know it's true –
  High speeds they can't defend,
For lack of thought will come to nought –
  Driving too fast round a bend!
Better to heed, a much slower speed,
  Just like your tortoise friend.

No need to shout and rush about
  When a quiet calm will do,
For arriving late is a better fate
  Than arriving in a stew.
No good will be done, no laughter or fun
  By an injured or clapped out crew,
So stop the race, or reduce the pace,
  Let the tortoise accompany you!

134

WEST COAST

A raging sea with angry climbing waves
  Crashing on the pointed jagged rocks,
The mighty power our greedy world so craves
  That the churning sea reluctantly unlocks.

Flying foam descends like drifting snow,
  Tossed upon a dark and cruel coast,
To filter back where it must ever go,
  Drawn backward by the secret tidal host.

Sailors know the anger of the sea
  And the dangers that are lurking there below,
The rhythm of the waves runs free,
  Taunting with its kindless ebb and flow.

Yet western seas can softly brush the shoreline,
  Among the sheltered coves and golden sands,
That look towards Atlantic's blue horizon
  That hides the western coast from foreign lands.

And so the wonder of this craggy coastline
  Is revealed with every pounding crashing wave,
As we gaze across the ocean to the skyline,
  We know this great protection that we have.

★ ★ ★

LAWN DAISIES

Next time the lawn has just been mown, why not examine one of those decapitated daisies – a miracle of construction – consider how many of these tiny miracles there are in this world of ours – year after year, created by a true mastermind. How clumsy our own inventions are by comparison with these.

MEMORY'S GIFT BOX

Our memories are an important part of our lives, and serve us in two very different ways. It enables us to put dinner in the oven at the right time, collect the children from school, take the dog for an essential walk and remember other people's birthdays that we would rather not forget. We do not realise how important this part of our memory is to our daily lives until it fails us in some way.

But memory has another value and purpose that we do not always fully appreciate until the years have had time to create a magic gift box of delights on which to draw whenever the fancy takes us, or when it can profitably be used to help a current situation.

Younger people who will not have yet had time to create such a store of memories, can often benefit from those who have had the experiences that create memories in the first place.

Not all memories are happy ones, but all will be valuable in knowledge, all have something to teach us, and time has a kindly way of softening the impact of unhappy memories and enhancing the more joyous ones for our benefit. Some will be big and bold, having travelled on a major road of life, whilst others wandered through the quiet lanes and footpaths of our existence. All will have played their part in time, all still have a part to play and be of great value in helping to create further memories for a coming generation. Memories are a gift beyond price.

AUGUST 17TH
A cure

THE ANTIDOTE

If loneliness is hitting you
    So that life is hard to bear,
Go and find a lonely soul
    And show them that you care.
You'll both have happy memories
    That will blossom as you share
The blessings of those happier times
    Towards tomorrow, without fear.

AUGUST 18TH
Tranquillity

SILENCE IS GOLDEN No. 8

In the velvet darkness of night, with soft moonlight tracing its path across still waters, the quiet stability of the stars that have guided for thousands of years – here is the golden silence of sleeping tranquillity.

AUGUST 19TH
High ideals

TOWARDS A BETTER WORLD

The babies cry,
And so do I –
Because of all their pain.
The old folk sigh,
And so do I,
When their loneliness remains.

The animals must wonder why,
And so do I –
They experience so much horror.
Mankind must try,
And so must I,
To ease the pain and sorrow.

Let the better world deny –
And so must I –
The power of evil thought.
Let love aim high –
And so will I,
Just as the Master taught.

AUGUST 20TH
Lest we stumble

REACHING FOR THE STARS may be a worthy and satisfying occupation, but we must beware the potholes at our feet.

137

AUGUST 21ST
The greater plan

THERE IS A REASON

When clouds are scudding through the sky,
Or sadness makes you want to cry,
Each is part of a greater plan,
There always is – a reason.

If sorrow wends its way to you,
If friends forsake or don't ring true,
Both blend into a greater plan,
There always is – a reason.

Our training in this earthly life,
Is often hard and full of strife,
But God controls the greater plan,
There always is – a reason.

And when the sun shines once again,
We know we'll always need some rain,
And Nature knows the greater plan,
There always is – a reason.

When our hearts are full of song,
And nothing makes the days go wrong,
This too is part of the greater plan,
And Spirit knows the reason.

AUGUST 22ND
A test of time

WARTS AND ALL

To know a friend is to love that friend, for if you don't like what you know, you are not friends. If you love a friend in spite of all you know or because of it, your friendship was made without your knowledge and before you came together – it was meant to be – and will stand the test of time and all adversity.

138

AUGUST 23RD
Compassion's gift

DOORWAY TO HEAVEN

If all the world would send a smile
　　Instead of bombs and tears,
And everyone could laugh awhile
　　Instead of hate and fear,
In place of horror, kindness given,
　　The pain all eased away,
The angels then could smile in heaven,
　　As we greet the joyful day
With happiness in every soul,
　　Compassion in every heart,
A peaceful world our final goal,
　　And now is the time to start.
For every thought of love we give,
　　Is a gem that's heaven sent,
The shining moments we could live
　　In this life that's only lent.
May every dark and cruel mind
　　See compassion's guiding face,
And learn the joy of being kind –
　　The entrance to heaven's grace.

★ ★ ★

AUGUST 24TH
A giggle surprise

　　　　　　　WHOOPS!

I think if I creep along behind,
He'll never know what I have in mind,
Or what mischief I might do,
If I could give a tweak or two!

139

THE DREAM

The human race can rightly seek its dream
    Of universal harmony and peace,
With nations joined as one great kindly team,
    That cruelty and pain shall one day cease.

When individual consciences are stirred,
    And ice floes never stained with the blood of seals,
And kindness joins in action undeterred,
    We'll see the light of love that it reveals.

When raucous sound of markets turn to song,
    And flesh is never turned to dying gore,
And people learn to sort the right from wrong,
    Then callous thought and action is no more.

In future times the dog can have its day,
    The donkey, horse and cat be unafraid,
The outstretched hand will soothe all cares away,
    Never more in anger to be laid.

When starving children weep no more in pain,
    And life on earth is adequately fed,
Mankind can lift its guilty head again,
    When everyone receives their daily bread.

With seas no longer red from harpooned whales,
    And pesticides no longer killing butterflies,
With curlews flying free o'er moors and dales,
    Mankind can see its way to be more wise.

When peaceful badgers trundle through the leaves
    Unmolested by the cruelties of man,
And deer can browse in peace amongst the trees,
    Mankind is getting near to God's own plan.

When greedy slaughter bows its shameful head,
    With cruelty an echo from the past,
And evil thought is well and truly dead,
    The human race can find its dream at last.

A HELPING HAND – a gift beyond price that costs us nothing but time.

RELIGION

Religious thinking is the greatest source of moral guidance ever invented. It is also the cause of more suffering and fear than any other. This is not the fault of religion itself, but the many interpretations that mankind has placed upon it through the years.

The numerous facets of religious thinking, originally designed to help and guide nationalities in various parts of the world, are sound enough to produce peace and happiness everywhere. But some of Mankind's inherent faults have wrongly used religions and caused misinterpretation. Greed and a lust for power and possessions triggers the intolerance, cruelty and inflated ego that have caused so much pain and sorrow throughout the world and years. The evil tortures and killing that have been perpetrated in the name of religion are testament enough to these facts. The blatant use of religions as an excuse for such behaviour is a terrible blot on the history of human endeavour.

Only people can redress the balance, only compassion and tolerance can provide the pathway, so that understanding and truth can prevail in the name of religion in the future. There are so many pathways to God – the one great power of love and integrity. The rest of us can only follow that example as best we may, and be ready to help all others even though their road may be different to our own. Religion can help us if we choose to let it do so, or we can misuse it at our peril without learning from the mistakes of the past, and each soul on earth has the opportunity to play its part on its journey through earthly life, so that compassion and true spiritual thinking can eventually lead the people of the whole world to a heaven on earth.

★ ★ ★

A HEALING PRAYER

May the giving and receiving
  Of God's own healing power,
Reveal to us the meaning
  Of Spirit's timeless hour
Of peace and harmony within,
  To erase the pain and sorrow,
May healing love this day begin,
  Bring sweet content tomorrow.

141

WAITING IN THE WINGS

The August gardens are ablaze with flowers, lifting hearts and minds that might otherwise have drooped like plants in need of life giving sun and rain. The second flush of roses shout defiance to the ebbing year, whilst great clumps of annuals – cultivated into glory by the wiles and tricks of Gardening Man – solicit gasps of admiration for their colourful and wild display. They do not know their days are numbered now that autumn lurks not so very far away. These flowers that have shone with riots of colour to please mere humanity must slip away to heaven's garden to delight the people there, for these flowers are too frail to withstand the test of cold and.time. Their man-made glory is no match for winter storms and weakened midday sun.

Yet here and there a flower grows that battles on regardless, not knowing how to die away completely, determined to show people how courage can live and conquer all adversity. The heartsease and the marigold, alyssum and daisy along with drawf nasturtiums will oft defy the colder days and shyly offer comfort from their cold and wintery beds.

They may have gone unnoticed amongst summer's gaudy bright display, but they were there, waiting for the moment when their modest perseverance is a welcome sight for human eye and recognition.

How like the flowers people are, for some will lift the hearts of the crowd with their colourful skills and outgoing nature, sometimes with a brash display, whilst others are standing in the wings of life, ready to uplift and bring a smile when all the rest have spent their strength and faded into insignificance – an observation and a lesson we wisely should not miss, less we overlook a valuable asset in our midst that can make the difference between sadness and a happy smile.

★ ★ ★

DETERMINATION

"Ah, human frailty, where is thy conscience and will to leap at duty with a smile?" It is not lost, but hiding in the cupboard we call determination, and we must seek it out and use it to good purpose, lest it crumble to dust for lack of air and use.

THE FIELD MICE AND THE BUTTERFLY

Two little field mice
   Were climbing up some stalks,
Setting off to meet their friends
   On little mousey walks.

"Hello" said the first one,
   "I'm feeling so forlorn,
Because I haven't seen you
   Around the buttercups and corn."

Soon they were achattering,
   Just like you and me,
When a butterfly came flitting by
   To see what she could see.

She sat upon a mousey ear
   To note their conversation,
When the other mouse espied her there
   And jumped with consternation.

The other mouse was then so scared
   It made her feel quite frail,
She knocked the butterfly for six
   By flipping up her tail!

The two little field mice
   Then felt very sad,
To see this lovely butterfly
   Looking limp and bad.

They sniffed around to help it,
   They poked it just to tease,
Until she flapped her wings a bit,
   And made the field mice sneeze!

So all three learnt the lesson,
   As the ancient saying goes,
We really must be careful
   Where we poke our nose!

SEPTEMBER

SEEING IS BELIEVING

SEPTEMBER

There's nothing quite so beautiful
   As September's golden hue,
There's nothing quite like footprints
   In the morning's cool moist dew.

No other month brings mystery
   That filters through sun rays,
The secrecy of morning mist,
   Changing to golden days.

Jewelled cobwebs dry their threads
   From fiery leaves of heaven's tree,
Late summer daisies tumble down,
   Cascading round the last sweet pea.

Walking down the silent paths,
   Hearing autumn's quiet cries,
By the sedum's rosy heads,
   Through a cloud of butterflies.

Splash of orange dash of red,
   The air is scattered with perfume,
That final thrust of energy
   From roses in their second bloom.

Twilight falling, autumn sun
   Dips his head in holy mass,
Shadows lengthen, tinged with blue
   And purple shades of Michaelmas.

SEPTEMBER 2ND
The choice

WORDS

Words have an importance in our lives almost beyond our imagination, and their effect often depends on the way we use them. We can win or lose any situation with the right or wrong use of words – we can make or lose friends, uplift a soul or knock it down – the choice is ours.

147

SEPTEMBER 3RD
Golden leaves

AS AUTUMN COMES

The autumn mist will gently shroud the hills,
And hide the fields where summer's ploughman tills,
Or send clear waters gushing through the mills,
And silence reigns where springtime's blackbird trills.

Golden leaves will toss and rustle as they will,
Autumn fruits will fall, their purpose to fulfil,
While butterflies will sleep and dream until
God's master plan of nature serves us still.

★ ★ ★

SEPTEMBER 4TH
Helping others

SERVICE

Service means different things to different people. For many it is something they have done regularly to their car, whilst for others it is something they demand quickly and efficiently in a shop, restaurant or bank. It may be a quick response to a telephone call when the vacuum cleaner goes wrong or the toilet springs a leak. Years ago, service meant a young woman going to work at the local 'Big House', often in very demeaning circumstances, for if she started on the bottom rung of the ladder, she was everybody's drudge for little pay and poor conditions – she was in fact a servant in the worst possible sense of the word because of the service she gave. Fortunately such situations do not often arise now, although we can still hear of the rich taking advantage of the poor, demanding too much service for too little pay and treating their servants in a demeaning way in attempts to 'Keep them in their place' – shadows of bygone days from which some people have not progressed.

Today we see service in a different light, we recognise it as helping others without thought of reward – giving instead of taking, for it is through service to others that we can make our own spiritual progress. Kindly thoughts and actions towards others, help where help is needed, these are the pathways of generosity and service that uplift both giver and receiver, these are the routes to true happiness and heaven – service with a smile.

148

FROM FROG

I'm just a little croaky frog
That likes to hide beneath a log,
To spring and jump out all agog
To tell you of this monologue.

I never mean to give a fright,
When human beings catch the sight
Of me jumping in full flight,
So I hope you understand alright!

I do a lot of good you see,
As I'm hopping round with glee.
But I have one little wish and plea
That people wouldn't eat poor me!

★ ★ ★

PERSONAL RESPONSIBILITY

It is all too easy to blame the circumstances in which we find ourselves for any adverse action that we may take. The fact remains, that some other folk would take different action under the same circumstances, and their reaction to those circumstances may be worse or better than our own.

Realization of these simple facts, reminds us that we are always personally responsible for our own reactions to the circumstances we are given. We may feel those conditions are thrust upon us whether we like it or not, or they maybe of our own choosing – we could have 'rushed in where angels fear to tread', but our reaction is always our own, and it is for each one of us to try and react in the right way – our conscience should be our guide to our personal responsibility.

SEPTEMBER STAR

Oh morning star, that hangs there so majestically,
   To brighten the eastern sky before the sun arrives
To take your task, and embellish it with rays
   So bright that you must fade, as now the human eye espies
The coarser beams that give us light throughout the days.
   Yet you have stood the test of time to give us hope
On each September morn since sky and earth began,
   With quiet prudence, to remind an erring world
That every soul has its own important part and place
   In the universe of life, that time has quietly unfurled,
To give frail human nature the courage to go on,
   With knowledge that power exists, beyond our comprehension,
To guide the human race with love and pure compassion,
   Blended to our souls by September's morning token
That shines now, and for all eternity,
   To fulfil a promise that will remain unbroken.

OUR KNOTTED IDEAS

Lambs were frisking in the field,
   A gambolling Spring display,
People watched and kindly smiled,
   With no thought of a later day.

And yet the day would soon draw near
   When their playful dance would cease,
The slaughter men would do their work,
   Dividing the flesh from fleece.

How can we grown-up human beings
   Tie compassion in such knots,
That we cannot see those happy lambs
   Are autumn time's lamb chops?

And now those autumn days are here,
   We must face the awful truth,
We condone death of an innocent life,
   And the lamb on our plate is proof.

THE ESSENTIAL INGREDIENT

In spite of our technology,
And all our modern trends,
Our happiness can still depend
On having loyal friends.

★ ★ ★

OUR COUNTRYSIDE is vital to the needs of us all. We should look at it with awe and leave it as we find it, leaving nothing behind that is foreign to it, take from it only pictures for our memories, and kill only a little of our own time while we appreciate its beauty.

★ ★ ★

MERRY GOLD

Summer days are shorter now,
Garden flowers are past their best,
Summer leaves fall from their bough,
Untidy in their autumn rest.

And yet among the twigs and rubbish,
Braving all the coming cold,
Determined that her joy will flourish –
A simple orange marigold.

A heartless hand may tear her roots,
Regarding her as common weed,
Crushing her beneath his boots,
Thoughtless of her power to seed!

And so her battle rages on –
Determined lady of the soil,
For though some people think her common,
Her cheerful face lifts hearts in style.

It is so easy in this life,
To overlook the hearts of gold
That struggle on through toil and strife,
Just like our merry marigold.

151

KINDLY HUMOUR

The world needs laughter, fun and games
    To ease the pain and sorrow,
A gentle humour kindly given
    Will brighten up tomorrow.

The gentle fun that cannot hurt
    Nor be a cause of tears,
Will give someone the strength to laugh
    As it travels down the years.

For laughing moments stay to live
    In memory's happy store,
To surface when there is a need
    And open humour's door.

So let us make a pact today,
    With the angels of gentle laughter,
That we will pass their message on –
    That a smile can ease disaster!

For humour is the spice of life
    When it is kindly meant,
A gift to use all through our lives
    That is truly heaven sent.

BUTTERFLIES HAVE EARS

Many a butterfly has fled
    Across the golfer's fairway,
Many a golf ball it must dodge
    'Cos the golfer can't see clearly,
But when the language gets quite tough,
    And the ball's stuck up a tree,
Remember, butterflies have ears,
    Just like you and me!

Determination

CLIMB EVERY MOUNTAIN

Most rock climbers and mountaineers indulge in these dangerous occupations simply because the rocks and mountains are there – a visual challenge that a few people feel obliged to accept. The will to overcome the difficulties and dangers is paramount to such people, the will to win being stronger than the fear of failure.

We are not all physically designed or capable of literally climbing the Everest's of this world, but we are all designed and capable of meeting and overcoming the spiritual challenges of life, the hills, the rocks and mountainous situations that we meet along the way. The more we try, the more likely we are to succeed. The guidance and support that we receive from Spirit, both strengthens and protects us through every challenge of life. We only have to ask and listen, and act accordingly. No mountain will ever look like a molehill but we will find we can climb even the highest and the roughest, with faith in the help that is there for us without fear or doubt. We can climb them just because they are there.

★ ★ ★

SEPTEMBER 15TH
Linked hearts and minds

FRIENDSHIP TRUE

Some things there are in earthly life
That never die or fade away,
True friendship, free of strain and strife
Will stay the course with proof, to say
The love of friends survives the night
Of sorrow, leading to a glorious day.

If distance proves apart awhile,
Or problems stretch this silken thread,
Then truth in friendship brings a smile,
And darker thoughts are truly dead.
True friends negotiate the miles
When minds and hearts are kindly led.

And when our lives on earth are done,
Tasks completed, knowledge gained,
The love of friendship still will come,
Reaching out to heal all pain.
For friendship true will join as one,
An everlasting joy ingrained.

HEAVEN'S DREAM

If every soul would love one more
    Than it has ever loved before,
And find a way to hate one less,
    And try to do its very best
To find the tolerance inside
    Its inner self, and so abide
By all the rules of kindly thought,
    And follow as the Master taught,
Then all the world would harmonize
    In songs of love to synchronize
Towards that hope of earthly peace,
    When greed and horror then might cease,
Compassion's power could reign supreme,
    Fulfilling the plan of heaven's dream.

THE TRAVELLED ROAD

When a life well lived with honesty
    Has travelled its allotted span,
It has earned a peaceful sanctuary
    According to God's own plan.

And so a worthy soul moves on,
    Free of pain and sorrow,
Every earthly task is done
    With courage towards tomorrow.

With duty done to both God and man,
    Walking life's many miles,
Lived in truth, as courage can,
    With kindly thoughts and smiles.

When such a soul has earned its place
    With kindness, love and sharing,
It finds the everlasting peace
    That heaven has been preparing.

154

BIRD OF PARADISE

Such wonders in the world we see,
Shrouded in mists of mystery,
From icy wastes to desert heat,
From wings and fins to pounding feet,
Or silent glade of flower and leaf
To stagger the mind in disbelief.

Large and small the wonders fly
To greet our ever watchful eye.
The majesty of a mighty tree,
The tiny insect wandering free,
The beauty of a flower in bloom,
Its colour, form and sweet perfume.

But nothing ever can compare
Or have a mystery quite so rare,
Or taunt our thoughts with fine display,
To teach us mortals how to pray,
With a heavenly name that will suffice
As a beautiful bird of paradise.

SILENCE IS GOLDEN No. 9

A quiet garden at dawn, has its own mist and mystery, for no-one ever heard the fall of dew upon the grass – here is a silence to be treasured.

SEPTEMBER 20TH
God knows!

READING THE SIGNS

When someone says 'I love you,'
    What do they really mean?
Could they mean this love is new,
    Or regret what might have been?

When someone says 'I love you,'
    It can mean so many things,
It might just mean they want you
    For the satisfaction that it brings.

If someone says 'I love you,'
    There's just one perfect rule,
For if their love is pure and true,
    They'll risk their life for you.

Yet love comes in many guises,
    And in varying degrees,
It's hard to read the signals,
    It's only God who *really* sees.

SEPTEMBER 21ST
Mixed-up thoughts

DELEGATING THE BLAME!

I overheard a scrap of conversation as I stood in the queue – "Did you hear the news last night? The world is a terrible place, how can God let these things happen?" For a brief moment I agreed with the sentiment – until I reflected that to blame God and the world for the state it is in, would be like blaming the car and its manufacturer when we can't start our vehicle because some mischief maker has put water in the petrol tank – or we had forgotten to get the petrol! How easy it is to delegate blame on to shoulders that can't or won't hit back!

TRAVELLING?

If we could use a bike instead of motor cars,
 Or rode on skates instead of on our bikes,
What a peaceful world we could envisage,
 Without a traffic jam within our sights.

On top of that we might dispense with skates,
 Replace them all with sprightly pairs of feet,
Our environment would seem to be quite safe,
 And our happiness should really be complete.

But what if all our legs wore short with walking,
 Whilst our minds were only dwelling on the stars?
We'd have to find a different way of travelling,
 And all go back to driving motor cars!

★ ★ ★

SEPTEMBER 23RD
Something in common

MOTHER'S PRIDE

The baby smiles, his tiny fingers grasp the loving hand held near, this long awaited son, so beautiful and good, prompts a tear of happiness to lurk there in his mother's eye.

Another mother sees an older son accomplishing a dream. Standing straight and tall as he receives the medal he has won for his school on the field of sport, he has overcome a disability, against all odds – he's won! She smiles and wipes a furtive tear of joy – this is her son.

A basket full of tiny shapeless squeaky things, a jumble of tails and heads, and four times as many legs and feet. Their mother looks towards her owner, eyes shining with achievement "Just look what I have here, these puppies are all my own."

The lioness breaks cover, pausing while her cubs catch up and cautiously emerge upon the world at large, to see what they have never seen before, and let that world admire this feline family. Their mother glances round with head held high as she presents her great achievement with such dignity and pride.

This strange mix of motherhood has something in common, a special kind of love – we call it Mother's Pride.

157

FOR THE YOUNGER GENERATION

Blest are those who try to win
    In truth and honesty.
Greater blest are those who find
    Success with true humility.

But those who know the way to use
    Their gift for helping others,
Have learnt to steer their souls through life
    In service to another's.

And those who share those gifts from God,
    And use their knowledge wisely,
Shine like stars to light the way
    For some who stumble blindly.

For some are born to teach and lead,
    While some are born to follow,
And you my friend may see the need
    For a greater strength tomorrow.

Many the times you'll have your doubts,
    Sometimes you'll be afraid,
And many the times you'll know you're right
    With decisions that you have made.

Just keep your sights on the distant stars,
    Ask for guidance to see you through,
Protection and courage each step of the way
    With purpose that's kind and true.

And as you wend your way through life,
    Maintain your high ideals,
For you are blest with the heavenly task
    That each new day reveals.

And you will find the love and strength
    To guide you on your way,
To use those gifts and knowledge gained
    For tomorrow's magnificent day.

THE MYSTERY OF LOYALTY

Loyalty is a very desirable yet strange quality that seems to defy adequate description. It can appear in the most unlikely places and yet fail to manifest where we could reasonably expect it. Friends from whom loyalty might seem a foregone conclusion may fail this crucial test, whilst people that we know only slightly can rise to the occasion when loyalty is needed. Sometimes a person we barely like will offer us loyalty in some dispute within an organization of work or play, for loyalty appears to spring from an acute sense of fair play and in many situations a deep knowledge of the difference between right and wrong.

At the same time, loyalty can be expressed towards someone known to be doing something that is not right, which could be explained by an emotional attachment towards that person rather than the indifference or even dislike that may be present in other circumstances. No wonder the quality of loyalty mystifies us so much.

When we pause to realise that animals also express loyalty, both in the wild state and in the domesticated conditions into which we have brought them, we have to accept that this quality of thinking has many more implications and possibilities than might appear on the surface of life. Many a dog or horse displays exceptional loyalty to its owner, probably prompted by affection in most cases, but it is certainly not unknown for them to be loyal to an owner who does not treat them at all well. Occasionally we hear of an animal that has pushed its efforts beyond all reasonable expectation in order to save an owner from danger, sometimes an animal forfeits its life in such a cause. This cannot be explained by an ignorance of the danger, for animals have a very well developed instinct that protects them from danger, even when ordinary knowledge is not present. In the wild state, loyalty is usually confined to the same species or family group, but it is still there.

A possible explanation of exceptional loyalty, is that there maybe a special rapport between two souls from a previous existence. When we accept that animals also have souls, it becomes clear that this explanation would be possible for them also, either between each other or in a relationship with a human personality.

Some souls maybe more advanced than others, giving them this increased knowledge of unselfishness and a greater awareness of the need for loyalty. It is a quality that the human race obviously shares with the animal kingdom. Maybe the human element could even learn something worthwhile about loyalty from its animal friends.

SEPTEMBER 26TH
Valuable memories

THE VOICE OF EXPERIENCE

There comes a time in most human lives, when experience and knowledge gained long ago are the main things remembered. Memory of yesterday's lunch and the whereabouts of a coat or hat have flitted off with easy abandon whilst a childhood memory of an unexpected kindness or an old thatched cottage in a country village remains clear and bright.

The younger generation despairs of these strange quirks of memory, not realising that yesterday's lunch doesn't matter now. They have not realised the value of those experiences of long ago, unwritten words that can be of interest, guidance and upliftment to those who care to listen to the voice of experience, for amongst the trivialities of yesteryear there will emerge a gem or two that can help posterity. That is why the older folk remember them.

SEPTEMBER 27TH
Flower knowledge

THE MASTERMIND

The summer now runs out of time,
    The flowers are past their summer prime,
The plants will fold away to sleep,
    Their tryst with nature they must keep.

How will they know when spring returns?
    To waken flowers, trees and ferns?
It maybe warmth or lighter days,
    Perhaps the Saint of gardens prays.

These can't apply to all that grows,
    For some can push through freezing snows,
There must be magic in the air,
    Or a mastermind to love and care.

It seems that we've no need to fear
    That flowers won't know the time of year,
For God has made a perfect plan
    That only flowers understand!

160

SEPTEMBER 28TH
Security

ROOTS

The roots of true friendship run deep and sure – they are the oak trees of emotion that can withstand the buffeting of life's elements and stand supreme in any kind of weather.

★ ★ ★

SEPTEMBER 29TH
Another giggle

SEEING IS BELIEVING

A pair of insects went for a walk,
And as they walked they'd laugh and talk,
Then they'd settle down for fun,
To kiss and flutter in the noonday sun.
A little time must pass away
Before they reach that special day,
When all things happen according to plan –
Our insects friends are pushing a pram!
It's the same old endless story –
Nature's plan of love and glory.
We know the power of the world's creator –
But insects pushing a perambulator?
This could surely never be,
But we *must* believe what we can see!

★ ★ ★

SEPTEMBER 30TH
The golden years

THE AUTUMN YEARS

People greet the autumn of their lives in so many different ways, depending on their past experiences, their hopes or fears for the future, their religious beliefs and current circumstances. Only one thing is certain – these golden years will depend very much on the thoughts and attitudes of each individual. For many, the autumnal colours and scents are the best time of the year, they prefer the quiet peace of achievement to the urgency and bustle of spring and the competitive anxieties of summer. Human attitudes and views of life reflect the seasons of the year as surely as the human life span itself. September ends in glorious triumph, to mirror those golden autumn years.

OCTOBER

OUR NOBLE HERITAGE – THE HORSE

The autumn story

OCTOBER

With fiery red and brilliant shining gold,
We gaze with wondering sorrow to behold
Each straggling flower, striving to grow old
With dignity, before the earth grows cold.

The silent slowing down of summer glory,
Renews each year the truth of autumn's story,
To rest before the springtime comes so surely,
Which winter's meditation proves entirely.

Some tired leaves give of themselves to earth,
To feed the soil and giving new flowers birth
To show the value of their dying worth,
And prove eternal life in next year's floral wealth.

The nipping teeth of early morning frost,
Or heap of leaves where whipping winds have tossed
The loveliness that grew and lived and lost,
All play their part and must not count the cost.

And so October wends its glorious way
Untidily through every autumn day,
And with its shaggy garden tries to say,
The time is near to rest, renew and pray.

OCTOBER 2ND
The striving counts

AIMING HIGH

Human effort that is aimed high will get nearer to perfection than when the target is lower set, but it is well to remember that nothing on earth is absolutely perfect – a rose has its thorns, and the bluest sky will eventually be studded by clouds, yet these will bring much needed rain that will in turn produce another rose with yet another thorn. The striving is never quite complete, nor yet the results of the effort, but we must always try to do our best and the results of aiming high will be rewarding to ourselves. It matters not what others think.

OCTOBER 3RD
Safe harbour

LOYALTY – the anchorage of friendship.

A ROAD TO HEAVEN

Silently he walked the miles,
  Lonely and misunderstood,
Scarcely could he climb the hill,
  Tired and weak through lack of food.

In his hand he held a life,
  Abandoned by another man,
Pleading eyes no longer bright,
  Gazed from the puppy in his hand.

And then a lady saw his plight,
  She gave him sustenance,
He smiled his thanks with sheer delight,
  And fed the life he'd found by chance.

Strengthened now, his way he trod
  Along the winding road,
Towards the love that he called God,
  That He might share his load.

The lady hurried after him,
  A tear slipped from her eye,
This man in lonely wandering,
  Had shared without a sigh.

"Come back" she said, "And I will find
  Some food for you as well."
"My lady you are very kind –
  May this baby with you dwell?"

She took the puppy to her heart,
  For she was lonely too.
The gentle stroke ere he depart,
  For the life that was so new.

And so three lives brushed quietly,
  Like ships that pass at night,
A puppy now with home and love,
  And two memories shining bright.

The mystery of Spirit's plan,
  The trails of chance encounters,
Are there for loving helping hands
  To use all God's endeavours.

And when all earthly life is done,
  And each has played their part,
The glory that each soul has won,
  Depends on a kindly heart.

OCTOBER 5TH
Brief enchantment

AUTUMN BEECH

October's beech of gold and flame
Putting the miser's hoard to shame,
Charms the eye and teases the mind,
Such golden beauty is hard to find.
With branches linking overhead,
A touching kiss twix gold and red
Creates a church of paradise,
From nature's trees and sound advice
Great columns rise in lancet form,
To linger when the autumn's gone
In lacy patterns 'gainst the sky,
Leaving us to question why
This glory that seemed ever near
Must drop away till another year.
Perhaps the magic would not stay,
If we could see it everyday,
Maybe enchantment must be brief
To appreciate the autumn leaf,
Perhaps the many joys of life
Mean so much more compared with strife,
When their welcome stay is short,
Like the beauty autumn brought.
October's glorious fiery beech
Maintains that balance we too must keep.

OCTOBER 6TH
A seventh sense?

FUN

A sense of fun is a gift to the human race so that hearts and minds may be lightened, strengthened and healed. But its purpose is only fulfilled when the fun is used in the right way – a kindly way. If fun is used to hurt or demean another it can be destructive and cause great distress, and a valuable gift is lost by misuse.

Animals also exhibit the gift of fun, especially when they are young, but many pet animals continue to demonstrate a sense of fun for most or even all of their lives. It is for each of us to share in the give and take of true kindly fun, so that this gift may for ever brighten the lives of all. Laughter is a great healer and strengthener, but it has to be prompted into action and received in good faith, by a kindly sense of fun.

167

THE GIFT OF SIGHT

How easily we take for granted
　　The ability to see,
How much pleasure would we lose
　　If we could never see a tree?

Could we visualise a butterfly,
　　Or understand a flower,
A tiger or the moon at night,
　　Or a honeysuckle bower?

How often do we *really* look
　　At any of these things,
Or use the gift of sight we have
　　And share the wonder that it brings?

It's clear we should be grateful
　　For the blessing of our sight,
And help the folk who cannot see –
　　Whose day is always night.

For God gave us the privilege
　　Of eyes that set us free,
And we can give in gratitude,
　　To those who cannot see.

OCTOBER 8TH
A sad situation

HUMANE BEINGS

Lambs that gambolled so happily and so prettily in the fields during springtime days, are nearing the end of their earthly lives, so that human beings may eat them. It seems very sad that so many people are not quite spiritual enough to qualify for that extra "e" that would make them into humane beings, so that thoughts could smile in the spring with a clear conscience.

BEETLES BEWARE

If I were a beetle,
   I wonder what I'd do,
If I saw a person coming
   With a large and ugly shoe?

I reckon I'd be real afraid
   In case it stepped on me,
Sometimes it's done on purpose
   I think you will agree.

If I were a beetle,
   I'd wish I had a voice,
So I could shout a warning,
   And so give the shoe a choice.

But not many shoes would bother
   To try and move away.
Their owners are too careless
   To let me live another day!

OCTOBER 10TH
Procrastination

UNDER THE CARPET

How easy it is to ignore the things we don't wish to hear or see. How much harder it is to deal with them when we finally have to face them. It is easy enough to brush undesirable situations under our metaphorical carpets, but we can be appalled at the mess that has accumulated through time when we finally have to look beneath the rugs of life and deal with those things we have left undone!

★ ★ ★

OCTOBER 11TH
A tiring emotion

ANGER is foolish and tiring, and it takes a lot of love to repair its damage.

169

OCTOBER 12TH
Life's reshuffle

THE CARD SHARPERS OF LIFE

So many problems of the world are caused by greed and lack of compassion. Most of the evils and imbalances of worldly conditions, from war to famine, can be traced to these two basic human faults in people whose sense of values have gone sadly awry, for they have cheated on fellow mankind and dealt some bad hands with the cards of life. Dishonest manipulation of truth is a sleight of hand and mind that can disguise evil and hide compassion. It is for detectives of kindly disposition to sort the true from the false, and by example show the card sharpers of life that greed, cruelty and dishonesty are wrong and unacceptable traits. People of greater understanding can help them towards a less selfish way of thinking and living, for only compassion can reshuffle our values into the proper order that would deal a kinder hand throughout the world.

OCTOBER 13TH
Life's contrasts

THE ORCHID AND THE DAISY

Supreme in quiet mystery,
  With a charm that's all her own,
A flower of perfect dignity,
  The finest ever grown.

Her perfection leads a pretty dance
  Among the simpler flowers,
A daisy wouldn't stand a chance
  Beneath the orchid bowers.

Yet a daisy too is perfect
  Within her own small way,
And lends a charm we can collect
  Through each and everyday.

But the majesty an orchid brings,
  Queen of all that she surveys,
Helps us strive for higher things,
  By the part in life she plays.

Yet still the daisy lends her charm,
  Her contrast is supreme,
For who would wish a daisy harm
  While she points us to a dream.

170

OCTOBER 14TH
Life's ocean

THE SEAS OF LIFE

Fear not the dervish waves and dashing seas
    That seek to mould the coast to shapes unknown,
Whipped to frenzy by a giant breeze
    That tries to be a gale in violence blown
To bend the strength of seamen, rocks and trees,
    Where frail birds have battled, won and flown.

The seas of life may toss us to and fro,
    Buffeting our minds with winds of change,
To shape our lives and thinking as we go,
    To seek and find some tasks in fair exchange
For the rise and fall of daily ebb and flow,
    That courage finds the strength to rearrange.

★ ★ ★

OCTOBER 15TH
Making decisions

LEST WE DON'T TRY

We must not judge – the Bible says – lest we ourselves be judged. Nevertheless, we have to make assessments. How else can we sort right from wrong, or make sure that compassion overcomes pain and cruelty?

★ ★ ★

OCTOBER 16TH
Just another giggle

FUN KITTEN

My halo isn't slipping,
In fact it's still intact,
It's just with fun I'm brimming,
'Cos I'm such a small wee cat!

But if I can find a ball of wool
To get all nice and tangled,
I think my halo might fall off,
And probably get mangled!

171

OCTOBER 17TH
At last

SILENCE IS GOLDEN No. 10

It's been a busy, noisy day – the baby's fretful with a cold, the supermarket clashed with the noise of trolleys and a screaming child that could not have its way. Some impatient motor horns yelled in a traffic jam, while two drivers argued when their bumpers touched. All the dogs in the neighbourhood seemed to find a reason to bark their disapproval. Nerves are taut, but now it's late, the darkness of night has slipped to the rescue, and the baby sleeps at last. Silence, once again is golden.

★ ★ ★

OCTOBER 18TH
Song of friendship

FRIENDSHIP'S WEATHER VANE

No matter what the weather,
   Be it sunshine, rain or gale,
Through winter frost or summer heat,
   True friendship cannot fail.

For the golden warmth of friendship
   Defies life's elements,
Brings forth the flowers of truth and trust –
   The values that make sense.

These moments come and fly away
   With every friendship meeting,
Like springtime flowers that yearly grow
   And renew true friendship's greeting.

The passing years can only smile,
   For no matter what life brings,
The weather vane of happiness
   Is the song true friendship sings.

★ ★ ★

OCTOBER 19TH
It's not the world!

THE DARK SHADOWS

There is nothing wrong with the world, it is only the fact that some of the people in it are so spiritually undeveloped, that their own density casts dark shadows of cruelty and pain.

A two sided risk

THE FIRE GAME

If we play with fire, we know there is a serious risk of getting burnt. When we play with the facts of life in the same irresponsible way we can so easily create much burning distress.

Some people actually seem to court dangers for themselves and may fail to realise the adverse conditions to which they are exposing themselves and others. Yet most people involved in such risky situations would probably display a self-righteous anger if someone else inflicted these risks on them.

Sometimes the fire game is played purely because of a need to prove something intangible within themselves. Perhaps they brought this need to earth with them, a challenge from a previous life, because the challenges are numerous, and on the physical level can range between risks on sea, land or in the air. The urge to gamble lurks beneath the surface of playing with fire, and may involve power, money, possessions or life itself. If moral issues are involved, then personal self-centredness may be a trigger and will almost certainly affect other people adversely.

Those who challenge life and circumstances for right and unselfish reasons provide the jam on the bread of life for the rest of us as they forge ahead in spite of every risk and warning. It would be a dull world without their ego, courage and enthusiasm for helping others. Theirs is the challenge and achievement, which has nothing in common with the fire game of selfishness and secret intrigue, for these are not bedfellows, they are not even companions, and do not speak the same language, whilst bravery against a challenge on behalf of a good purpose can be a special kind of spirituality.

★ ★ ★

OCTOBER 21ST
Just around the corner

WHEN ALL ELSE FAILS there is still God. Where there is God there is hope, and where there is hope there is courage and peace of mind. None of them are too difficult to find.

OUR NOBLE HERITAGE – THE HORSE

Throughout Great Britain's history
  Of power, grace and shame,
There is one majesty of life
  That rises without blame,
Exemplary in the service given,
  Yet modest in its fame.

Proud battles have been fought and won
  Upon his broad strong back,
With heavy loads he's pulled and strained
  Along rough road and track,
Yet gently carried the child and weak,
  And overweighted pack.

With grace and patience he has served
  His master through the years,
No anger or cheap greediness
  Or unworthy hate or fears,
Just friendly courage freely given
  Through both happy times and tears.

Straight the furrow he has ploughed
  Through field and life alike,
He's towed the longboat through canals,
  Suffered the whip and brutal strike,
Dragged the timber, sown the seed,
  Proudly knowing the wrong from right.

The power behind each earthly throne
  Carried forth without remorse,
From tiny Shetland to Gentle Giant,
  Giving service without force
Is mankind's greatest heritage,
  The noble, majestic horse.

OCTOBER 23RD
Our own contribution

AN INEXPENSIVE ANSWER

COMPASSION and unselfishness are the two great needs of the world. Everyone can contribute, and these things need cost us nothing but just a little time and thought.

OCTOBER 24TH
A silent prod

THE WORRYING SILENCE

It can be aggravating to have a noisy child, a barking dog or someone that clatters around whenever they are busy. Even a nice neighbour can be bothersome if they play loud music or have the habit of singing loudly out of tune!

Yet it's strange how we start to worry when such aggravations stop! We immediately fear there must be something wrong. Of course it could sometimes be that there is something wrong with us – intolerance perhaps? Or maybe we have just allowed ourselves to become a little fraught, but at least we care enough to be concerned at the unaccustomed silence. Hopefully we care enough to investigate it.

★ ★ ★

OCTOBER 25TH
A flight of fancy?

A POSSIBLE HEAVEN?

There is a woodland by a lake,
  Where wild birds come, their thirst to slake.
Where people fly with grace and ease,
  And bluebells grow on fairy trees.

There's a meadow by a brook,
  Where barn owls sit to read a book.
Where gentle starlight greets each day
  To brighten every wanderer's way.

This place is full of lovely things,
  Where kings are tramps and tramps are kings.
Where kindly people share their deeds,
  To give the erring world its needs.

Here, daytime mixes with the night,
  All is gentle, pure and bright.
Babies sit in pixie prams,
  And gentle lions lie with lambs.

This heaven is not far away,
  For you can touch it if you pray
For peace upon your naughty earth,
  That love may give it second birth.

175

YOUTH OF THE YEARS

The youth of every generation
Is our hope for a better world,
The task of the old is to guide the young,
And the young to learn from the old.

But the old can also learn from the young,
For *there* lies the strength that is cast,
The future is theirs, they must make their mark
As the old folk did in the past.

But progress must be in the name of heaven,
The best of the old not lost,
The best of the new be kind and true
Or the future must count the cost.

The youth of the passing years of time
Have made both beauty and scars,
But when there's more of the true than the false
They are building a road to the stars.

★ ★ ★

October 27th
The past and the future

TIMELESS MEMORIES

Memories of springtime with its fresh new hope and upliftment, help us face the coming winter days, when nature wisely sleeps along with some of the animal kingdom.

It's easy to recall bright green leaves massed on oak and ash, the hands of leaves unfurled by the horse chestnut tree, and mists of almond blossom that enchant our tired gaze, as it imitates the decoration on a lady's hat of a bygone age. These memories enrich our lives as darker days come relentlessly towards us. They will also remind us that spring will follow winter, and renew again the optimism of nature with her stars of celandine, violets quietly peeping out from clumps of leaves, sudden bursts of primrose flowers on wayside banks – snuggled amongst the springtime grass.

The grand spectacles of spring and its small and gentle surprises, all serve to give us encouragement and hope when other seasons may fail. It is for us to let our memories wander back and find the strength to forge ahead.

SPECIAL FRIENDS

Truly reliable friends are not always easy to find. Such a relationship demands implicit trust, unselfish love, and an instinctive linking of minds that must compete with the diverse responsibilities and problems of daily life. It is small wonder that so many friendships stagger or even fail under such pressures. Those friendships that rise above the difficulties are treasures for which to be truly grateful.

Yet there are other friendships where unselfish trust is a natural instinct, and any problems are of a very different nature, and more concerned with language difficulties than uncertainty of motive or loyalty. Anyone can benefit from such a friendship, and experience the courage, devotion and trust of man's best friend – the dog. It asks no questions, knows no deceit, and will guard or even give its life for its human friend. What more can be given or asked by any friend? Anyone who has known pure friendship of any kind is privileged beyond the hopes and dreams of many, because it is a secret knowledge of the heart and mind that can only be expressed as loyalty and love – special friends that are treasure indeed.

OCTOBER 29TH
A golfing trial with a smile

LOST BALL

When the ball flies far and wide,
Then hides beneath the gorse,
It's time to smile I must confide,
For officially, it's lost!

So if the pin is not in view,
And neither is the ball,
Then you will know just what to do,
surrender point – and ball and all.

So if you have a golfing day,
When each hole is just a trial,
And nothing seems to go your way,
Just wave the flag – and smile!

SPARE TIME

Modern technology helps us to carry out so many daily tasks so quickly, that theoretically we should have a great deal of time to spare. It does seem a pity that so much of this spare time becomes entangled in fruitless occupation or selfish acquisition, when there is so much that is really worthwhile waiting to be done. Spare time used wisely and with kindly intent, can prevent a great deal of suffering for both people and animals.

Many people do possess the wonderful spark of compassion together with the positive will and determination to make full use of it, so that their spare time improves many other lives. Their reward is in the happiness they find in the course of their activities as they help others. Such people do not have spare time for either fruitless occupation or selfish acquisition. In fact, they do not have spare time.

★ ★ ★

THE COMING OF WINTER

Nature now prepares her winter sleep,
Spreads her leaves, the summer warmth to keep
And make the bed for blanket snows so deep,
To cosset the plants as to their rest they creep.

Spring buds are neatly tucked away,
To weather the storms of a winter day,
And nestle themselves from the wild affray,
Keeping harsh winter gales at bay.

Red autumn berries greet the frost,
To say that summer will not be lost,
But merely sleep in branches tossed
By winter's wild and windy host.

And so God's winter settles down,
To rest the world's poor worried frown,
Yet from that sombre white and brown
Creates a perfect rainbow gown.

For while all nature dozes in her rest,
And sunny days are just a welcome guest,
We know that spring will come with joy and zest,
To clothe the land again with all that's best.

NOVEMBER

A GOLDEN GIFT

NOVEMBER 1ST
A garden of rest

NOVEMBER

November's garden rests awhile,
Untidily she hides her smile
In knowing summer's task is done,
And rest will come to every one
Of nature's plants and fine display,
That lifted hearts with fine array,
Through all the months of recent past,
To bring them peace and rest at last.

NOVEMBER 2ND
Is anybody there?

COINCIDENCE

Most of us at sometime or other, have experienced a strange fortuitous train of events that leave us feeling bemused and lucky – a sequence of events that we choose to call coincidences, without stopping to think what this really means, still less much gratitude for the help these situations often are to us.

This little trail of unexpected events that dovetail so neatly together to our advantage, suggests a guiding mind beyond any earthly source, even though very earthly people may be used to bring the plan to fruition. For plan it quite obviously is, defined in our dictionaries as a sequence of events that do not appear to be connected, and yet are dependent on each other to produce a specific result. Spirit at work perhaps? No-one has ever found a better explanation, for it is useless to call it 'luck', because we are then faced with trying to explain the source of that as well! It is a happy solution to the mystery, to believe there is someone there looking after our needs with a situation that we could not organise for ourselves – and who could prove us wrong?

NOVEMBER 3RD
A precious thought

FREEDOM OF THOUGHT is the greatest freedom of all, for it is true freedom of the mind.

NOVEMBER 4TH
Nature ignored

THE BALANCE OF NATURE

All life on earth is part of the balance of nature, and mankind is an integral part of that balance. It is therefore puzzling that so many people seek to destroy that balance, or at the very least use it so carelessly, that the whole structure becomes at risk.

So many choose to ignore known facts concerning this balance. The indiscriminate use of chemicals and the pollution of the very air that we breathe are but two obvious examples.

Overpopulation by the human race coincides with the persecution and destruction of much wildlife, which furthers the imbalance of nature. Meanwhile the use of unnatural practices to increase human population, and animals as well when it seems to suit homo sapiens – farm animals for example – only guides this unbalanced thinking into worse situations as time goes on.

When mankind learns to work *with* nature instead of trying to fight her natural concepts, perhaps we can restore some of the balance of nature on which we all depend.

★ ★ ★

NOVEMBER 5TH
A mystery smile

A GOLDEN GIFT

A friend gave me some flower seeds –
She knows a gardener's special needs.
Planted in a flower pot,
The label then she quite forgot.
The plants grew up without a name,
It really did seem quite a shame.
I was wondering what to do
With these plants that grew and grew,
First a foot and then two more,
I nearly lost count of the score!
Up they went towards the sky,
Until they reached just ten feet high.
Then the flower buds were forming,
Until one very special morning –
There they were in bright array
To make a very special day.
Through seeds of kindness from a friend,
These smiling faces came to lend
Their golden rays to cheer my way –
The sunflowers beamed their bright display.

182

NOVEMBER 6TH
A woof of a smile

A CANINE CONVERSATION

Said the Spaniel to the Yorkie,
  "How come you are so sharp?
It seems you hear the slightest sound –
  Even after dark."

Said the Yorkie to the Spaniel,
  (After careful observation),
"Our ears are very different shapes,
  An important consideration.

Mine are stuck up very straight,
  They've developed through the years,
Whilst you are wearing curtains
  Draped all around *your* ears."

"No need to laugh" the Spaniel said,
  "For *I've* got a sharper nose,
And I can sniff out anything,
  No matter where it goes.

And don't forget that people,
  With all their silly fears,
Share that awkward trait with me,
  They often have cloth ears!"

NOVEMBER 7TH
Two halves = one whole

PEACE IN OUR TIME?

If half the world were tolerant,
  And the other half were kind,
Peace would then be relevant,
  For all the world to find.

NOVEMBER 8TH
A valuable commodity

THE RIGHT WORDS at the right time have a value beyond price.

NOVEMBER 9TH
Raising our sights

OUR TASK

If it has a nervous system, it can feel pain. If it can feel pain it should be treated kindly, and we are the ones who must do it. Fear, mutilation and killing need not be inflicted on other life in the name of war, sport, experiment and food, nor should these have the acquiescence of the human race. To raise our sights beyond this degradation is a continuous task throughout our lives, a task that once attempted, will gradually raise our spiritual progression towards peace of mind and God.

★ ★ ★

NOVEMBER 10TH
A yell of a smile

HELP

What's that lady doing
   Standing on a chair?
There must be something brewing
   'Cos she's tearing at her hair.

I wish she'd stop that screaming,
   I must cover up my ears,
I hope she isn't dreaming
   Of nasty creepy fears.

She's looking up to heaven,
   Then looking down at me,
That's another yell she's given,
   Whatever can she see?

People are such funny things
   To have around the house,
I s'pose it's 'cos they're human beings,
   That they fright' a poor wee mouse!

184

NOVEMBER 11TH
"Lest we forget"

IN LOVING MEMORY

If every flower that ever grew,
    Were entwined into a wreath,
It would encircle all the world,
    For those who died for their belief.

If all religious thought would lend
    True tolerance and peace,
Those martyrs won't have died in vain,
    As war and suffering cease.

NOVEMBER 12TH
Selection

IN OUR OWN TIME

We always have time to do the things we really want to do. The other things
have to wait their turn.

NOVEMBER 13TH
Different ideas

VIEWPOINT

However much you'd like to change
    Another's point of view.
Remember please that their ideas
    Maybe quite valid too.

A sudden change may have no soil
    Where we our seeds can sow,
Whilst gentle learning we may find,
    Will help the flowers grow.

185

A CHILD IN CARE

A child in innocence is born
　To wend its way through life,
And teach its soul the mysteries
　That come through joys and strife.

A parent voice of loving care,
　Can guide a child's soul
Towards a happy future life,
　And fulfil its Karmic role.

But raucous sounds of anger raised
　As disciplinary measure,
Can bruise the mind and wound the thoughts
　That are memories for the future.

Each child will bring to earthly life,
　Some tasks it must perform,
To guide the soul towards its God
　Through the lessons it can learn.

Some souls may bring a special task,
　To help a dark humanity,
Rising above the dross of life,
　Towards a bright eternity.

And so we find a baby soul
　Born with gentle innocence,
Grow to strength and leadership,
　And give the world some recompense.

Thus we see the need to give
　Patient, loving care,
To every soul that comes to earth,
　No matter when or where.

For in our charge a life could be
　Intended for a greater plan
For higher work than we can see,
　So we must do the best we can.

186

NOVEMBER 15TH
The aftermath

SILENCE IS GOLDEN No. 11

Parties can be fun, bringing together people of like mind to enjoy and share the music, laughter, food and wine. But now the guests have gone, and all that remains is the washing up, the surplus food that will take days to consume – and the golden silence of memory.

★ ★ ★

NOVEMBER 16TH
Versatile kindness

THE MEASURE OF THOUGHT

A kind thought is a measure of love,
　　Any size, any height, any length,
It can make dreams come true,
　　It can be old or new,
Its value lies in its own strength.

A kind thought is a gift from the heart,
　　A generous offering of time,
It can halt a cruel act,
　　Or turn hopes into fact,
And even make other folk kind!

★ ★ ★

NOVEMBER 17TH
Unhappy for some

LET US REMEMBER

Soon the festive season will be lifting our spirits, people will be dancing, opening presents, eating and drinking in celebration of a birth many years ago. In the midst of the happy laughter, let us not forget that suffering is also a part of the celebration for many animals. The battery hens that laid the eggs for Christmas cakes – caged and unable to stretch their wings or scratch around the earth as they were meant to do. Let us not forget the poultry that have lived out their short lives in cruel cramped conditions, often injured or debeaked or never seeing the light of day. Let us not forget the pigs that have lived in crates unable to turn around until released by death, so that people can enjoy ham sandwiches as part of the celebration. Let us remember that such suffering need not be, and would shock and grieve the man whose birth is celebrated with these sacrifices. Let us remember to try and phase out the cruelty and replace it with a kind and worthy celebration of which we need not be ashamed.

187

NOVEMBER 18TH
A safe combination

THE KEYS OF HEAVEN

There is a bunch of master keys that can open all doors to true happiness and heaven, and once the code is known, anyone can use these keys. The problems arise when people wrongly interpret the code – they might for instance want to open those doors for selfish reasons of their own, so that the keys cannot work properly. Under these circumstances, those doors will not only remain locked, but the person wrongly using the keys may deceive other people about their intentions and cause them great distress. Some people can even deceive themselves with their supposed intentions, but an honest approach can quickly get them on to a better pathway – self confession is always good for the soul, and is a valuable guide to more spiritual thinking in the future.

We are all on this earth plane to learn, the quicker we assimilate such forward thinking, the sooner we will realise we have found the code for happy living – the keys to heaven. They really are not difficult to recognise once our motive is sincere – they are simply compassion, kindness, love and spirituality.

NOVEMBER 19TH
Wandering kindness

SHARING LOVING THOUGHTS

The peaceful love of spirits tending
Anxious souls on mother earth,
Bring the hope that they are lending
To every child of earthly birth.

If your sky is dark and gloomy,
If your feet slip on the rocks,
Take the hand of hope, and truly
Trust that God will lead His flocks.

But if your sky is bright and sunny,
Shining like a bright midday,
Share your feast of milk and honey
With those who pass along your way.

Thus the happy deeds of kindness
Multiply and wander far,
Cheering, clearing all the sadness,
Twinkling with the brightest star.

188

THE MAGIC OF MUSIC

Music has a power and quality that is all its own. It can uplift us to heights of emotion of which we have not dreamt. It can make us dance or march with impunity. It can steady frayed nerves or drive us to distraction. It can lead a crowd to a glory of appreciation or a frenzied stampede where brain power is lost to dark primitive instincts. We can receive music via a beautiful human voice, a bird in full throated song, an instrument well played upon, the soft gurgle of a bubbling stream or a softly sighing wind.

It is the receiving human ear and soul that determines our reaction to music. Some will respond to flowing tones that are in tune with kindness and peace, whilst at the other extreme, the human ear may respond to a discordant cacophony of sound that reflects utter confusion in daily life and thinking. Music has the magic power to cure discord or enhance a tuneful mind. It is for each individual to use the magic of music in the right way for the soul's progression.

★ ★ ★

HELPING FRIENDS

If sorrow knocks upon the door of life,
    Do not fear the lonely grief and tears that start,
For they are part of nature's healing hand,
    Heaven's gift to soothe an aching heart.

The cleansing tear will clear the path ahead,
    To make the walking easier with a smile,
As friends in Spirit lend a greater strength,
    To help you travel through this darker mile.

Seek in the quiet comfort of the night
    The peace of mind these friends can offer you,
For they are there to say you're not alone,
    As they give you help and comfort that is true.

Another point of view!

A FLOWER WEPT

There they were, all sitting there,
　With happy smiling faces,
Till someone came who didn't care
　For pansies in their places.

In went the fork without a sigh,
　To burst a pansy dream,
Tell me, did they really cry?
　I'm sure I heard a scream.

Tossed willy-nilly in a barrow,
　Their roots all naked shown,
Faces bruised by a gardener fellow
　Who cannot hear their moan.

Thrown onto a compost heap,
　Buried alive in soil,
Their little faces tried to peep
　Last looks at earthly toil.

Why can't a pansy fade away
　Like the decent lives they are,
And live to smile another day
　Away from a gardener's war.

A pansy could live in a drinking glass
　Until her task is done,
When natural death can come at last,
　When the quiet smile has gone.

May pansies find a life to live
　With gardener folk who know,
That pansies serve in life to give,
　As their smiling faces show.

NOVEMBER 23RD
Hard to find

If PERFECTION were easy to obtain, it would not be so rare, and would therefore lose its value.

190

NOVEMBER 24TH
It's worth the effort

PERSEVERANCE

If failure meets your first attempt at something that's worthwhile, always keep
on trying, and do it with a smile!

★ ★ ★

NOVEMBER 25TH
For better or worse

THE WINDS OF CHANGE

The winds of change go flying by,
Scattering rubbish far and wide,
Clearing old and troubled thoughts,
The ones we're always trying to hide.

The winds of change bring something new
To meet the challenge of modern times,
Yet draw upon the old and tried,
It is for us to read the signs.

For old and new share one true fact,
Each harbours good and bad,
And we must sort the right from wrong,
Lest the sighing winds be sad.

For every change is not a help
To an erring human mind,
But the best of all the old and new
Make the winds of change more kind.

★ ★ ★

NOVEMBER 26TH
A nonsensical truth

EGG FLIP

It's easy enough to be happy
    When the world seems a wonderful place,
But the people worthwhile,
    Are the ones who can smile
When they find they've got egg on their face!

191

THE NEGATIVE ENEMY

Negative thinking is the world's main non-event, yet by the extent of its own volume it is being remarkably successful in holding back progress in almost every field of endeavour. So many thoughts, actions and ideas are accepted as progress until time reveals the disappointments because negativity has misrouted the original. Thus the negative side of almost every human endeavour negates many of the advantages. However wonderful an idea or discovery may be, someone somewhere will find a wrong use for it, creating all sorts of problems – physical, material and moral, often affecting thousands, even millions of people.

In ordinary daily life, fear and uncertainty prevent the fruition of many a kindly thought and action, as negative thoughts infiltrate the minds of millions of people all over the world. The result is pain and unhappiness on a vast scale. The positive thinkers of this world are too few and far between, they are often feared, frequently mocked, yet their own philosophy of life can uphold them through all adversity and criticism.

Some positive thinkers are prompted by wrong motives, perhaps greed is their most powerful driving force, which by its very nature negates the positive original thinking, thus we find even positive thinkers being driven into negativity by their own darker motives. When a positive thinker casts his or her thoughts in the wrong direction – chaos results, and can be recognized in history as the evil result of a positive thinker on the wrong track of life, using their power and knowledge of positive thinking to destroy instead of the true progress they are in a position to achieve. Such leaders through history demonstrate for us the power of the negative enemy, which today could be so easily overcome with truly spiritual positive thinking.

If only more people would pause to consider ways in which they could accomplish something worthwhile rather than reasons why they shouldn't try, a phase of positive right thinking could be set in motion that could eventually scatter the negative thoughts, that by their weight of numbers are currently destroying so much happiness, worthwhile effort and progress. It is something in which every single person can play a part, and the first to benefit will be those who first put action into their thoughts and begin to think positively towards a better kinder world and life for all.

NOVEMBER 28TH
A few indigestible facts

SUPERIORITY

Have we really any good reason to consider ourselves so superior to the animal kingdom? Most species do not kill their own kind, something that occurs regularly with the human species. Animals do not torture merely for the sake of it or their own self-aggrandizement or greed. The only time we witness greed amongst the animals is directly associated with food especially in times of hardship, when it is part of their own survival mechanism, whereas the human species can become greedy out of sheer covetousness or inflated ego, which has nothing in common with actual survival, although we too are part of the animal world.

Pet animals are adept at reading the minds of their owners and are able to understand some of their owner's language. They clearly have the ability to think and reason for themselves, and also use the power of telepathy and body language to convey their own thoughts and needs to their owners. Animals are far better at telepathy than most human beings, they are more patient, tolerant and forgiving, and most people could profitably learn from their example.

Our knowledge of technology is obviously far superior, it is in fact entirely the achievement of human beings, who, having accomplished this feat of knowledge, promptly misuse much of it for their own ends, often in a way that is detrimental to the animals as well as others of their own kind. When we take just these few facts into consideration we are left to wonder how on earth we coined the idea that we are so superior.

NOVEMBER 29TH
Renewed hope and help

NIGHT AND DAY REFLECTIONS

The velvet night sky wanders in
And shelters me from fears within.
The morning bright sky filters through
To bring me hope and joys anew.
Make the most of each new day,
Help those in need who pass your way.

COUNTING THE YEARS WITH GIGGLES

One two three four,
　　What the heck am I counting for?
Two four six eight,
　　Watch me jump a five-bar gate.
Nine ten eleven twelve,
　　Into the kitchen I will delve,
There I'll raid the captain's fridge
　　For a pale pink sausage and a dark brown fig.
Thirteen, fourteen, fifteen now,
　　I'm off to milk the farmer's cow.
Now I'll count to twenty seven,
　　And all the people on the road to heaven
Through speeding on the motor way,
　　They chance their arm and the time of day,
But when I get to thirty-one,
　　This silly little ditty will be done,
For that's my lot as I can't count more,
　　When I've reached my limit at thirty-four.
But I hope that you have had some fun,
　　While I try to get to ninety-one.
If I succeed to ninety-two,
　　I hope you'll reach the same age too,
And if by chance we reach three figures,
　　We'll raise a toast to nonsense giggles.

★　★　★

DECEMBER

A RUGGED COASTLINE

DECEMBER

A robin trills his winter song
To help the frozen days along,
The holly berries sparkle there,
They have no silly grudge to bear.
But man must learn the secret rue
That holly has its prickles too,
In spite of beauteous glossy green
That brightens up our winter scene.

A Christmas rose may dare to breathe
The crispy air – and seek to weave
Pale sunshine into garment rare,
Bright golden garlands for her hair.
December's garden sleeps in peace,
Renews her strength – will never cease
To bring the joy of spring again
With wild flowers and leafy lanes.

DECEMBER 2ND
It's nice to be warm

COLD WORDS have no purpose except to hurt. Warm words can melt a frozen heart.

DECEMBER 3RD
Kind thoughts

CHRISTMAS GIFTS

Thoughts of many gifts and giving
    Come again at this time of year,
Along with the fun, the food and wine
    As Christmas time draws near,
But let us not forget the roots
    Of this celebratory cheer,
Let kindness be a Christmas gift,
    And a freedom from want and fear.
For the Christmas message really says
    "Let compassion now appear" –
A gift that's wrapped in many deeds
    And kind thoughts everywhere.

A RUGGED COASTLINE

A raging sea, surf flying high,
   White as driven snow,
Meeting fearlessly the rocks
   That are waiting there below.

Those jagged rocks snarl angrily,
   Challenge the churning sea,
The foam flies high, caught by the wind
   That flings it wild and free.

And yet the elements will change,
   The sea can calmly flow,
Caressing the cruel rocks of pain,
   And dancing to and fro.

A quiet murmur soothes the mind,
   As nought else ever will,
Beckoning the unwary on,
   Disguising the power to kill.

And so the sea's two sides are shown,
   Working in harmony,
A rhythm of life to soothe the soul,
   With the power of eternity.

★ ★ ★

DECEMBER 5TH
A risky giggle

MOUSE FUN

What a lovely puss to play awhile,
But I've teased her to no avail,
She just sits there with that snooty smile,
So I think I'll just tweak her tail!

198

THE GENTLEMAN

He doffed his hat that wasn't there,
Because indeed his head was bare,
But his gentle mind and kindly thought
Reflected what the Master taught,
For the gentleman that passed this way
Nodded and smiled and said "Good-day,"
He'd trod the earth many times before,
Knew every beauty and every flaw.
He sought to remedy the pain,
And lift the fallen up again,
He helped when something went all wrong,
Brightened a life with deed and song.

He fought for peace throughout the world,
The flag of love he had unfurled.
Some people scorned his ragged dress,
They did not know that he could bless
Their daily lives with kindly deeds,
And sow the magic power of seeds
Of loving thought and kindly action,
Phasing out the cruel faction –
In other peoples' daily lives,
Lived with guns or wordy knives
That maim and cut and bring dark sorrow,
Clouding hopes for a bright tomorrow.

The manner of this kindly gent,
Will travel on – it's only lent
To teach an erring world to think,
Prevent it getting out of sync
With nature's song of birds and trees,
Rivers, hills and tossing seas.
This gentleman can lead the way
Towards an ever brighter day,
And shows a kinder way to live,
Teaching others how to give.
With kindly love within his soul
He draws the picture for us all.

A variety of hats

FRIENDSHIP travels many miles on its journeys around the world, wearing a different hat for every circumstance and occasion.

DECEMBER 8TH
A strange celebration

TURKEY TALK

As we accept that the animal kingdom have brains, we must accept that they can think. In which case, it is worth wondering what Turkeys think about Christmas. Even if their thinking does not go that far, their instincts must give them cause for concern, because animals seem to possess more of this particular gift than most human beings. In the case of Turkeys, they might be better off without that instinct at this time of the year, then they would not experience the fear they must now know, until the very last moments of life. They would only know the physical pain and distress. The human race ought to be able to do better for them than this. Do we really need to inflict pain and kill to celebrate the birth of a man of peace, a man who taught love and compassion?

★ ★ ★

DECEMBER 9TH
Golden smiles

WINTER JASMINE

Showers of jasmine's winter gold,
   Cascading to the earth so cold,
Glinting in the morning sun
   Winter's pride of place she's won.

The birds that herald daily dawn,
   Rise above the misty morn,
To wake and cheer a sleeping world,
   For nature cannot be deterred.

The jasmine tossing in the wind,
   Shaking hoar-frost from her mind,
Stirs the sleeping gardener's hand,
   Lest nature serve her reprimand.

If we could travel life's own miles,
   With winter jasmine's golden smiles
Touching every human face,
   Our world would be a happy place.

A WEIGHT WATCHER'S LAMENT

When I really try to be
Fit and slim as a sapling tree,
Something always will go wrong,
And bring about a sad wee song.

When the pounds all disappear,
And fluent movement comes to bear,
And I should be all fairy light
It seems that I don't feel so bright.

The sparkle seems to hide away,
And won't come back until the day
When bulges reappear all round,
And happiness is pound for pound.

When walking up a hill I pant,
And move around like an elephant,
I feel as happy as a lark,
Although to fly is not my mark!

I've cycled miles on the bedroom floor,
Bent and danced till my joints are sore,
I've counted calories every day,
There's nothing left to do but pray!

Why is it that, I once was slim,
With every part of me so trim,
While pounds now cling and firmly hold –
At least I now don't feel the cold!

Sometimes I think I will give up
The fight to be like a one year pup.
Perhaps true fitness will not come
Till heaven is my happy home.

For no-one can be heavy there,
Nor be clumsy, or despair,
For they would fall right back to earth –
Sheer weight would give them second birth!

Perhaps I'll settle for half-way,
And live to laugh another day,
Just semi-fat I think will do,
That others may laugh with me too.

Every life should have some fun,
Cheer and smiles for everyone.
If I succeed by being fat,
Then that's my line – and that is that!

201

The road to a tranquil mind

THE CRY OF THE ANIMALS

Through the years of mankind's living history,
    And his battle with his unrelenting fate,
We trace a strange unanswered mystery,
    His ability for cruelty and hate.

Through the years of dark and toilsome living,
    And trying – often vainly – to be good,
There seems to be a weakness in our learning
    Of the kinder, gentle, understanding mood.

Animals of the world have gleaned first hand,
    With every torturous sound of scream and sigh,
The pain inflicted recklessly by man
    Who ignores the quiet appeal and haunting cry.

Our double standards now must die away,
    Never more a trust to be betrayed,
That animals may see the smiling day
    When the cruel hand of man has paused and stayed.

When slaughter is a nightmare of the past,
    And human beings are tranquil in their minds,
And compassion reigns supreme in every heart,
    Then animals will know the love that binds.

When guns no longer spread their fear and pain,
    And blood will never more stain Arctic sea,
Mankind will rise above his cruel shame
    And shine, because all life will then be free.

When traps and cudgels sink into obscurity,
    And ill-used whips and sticks are ancient history,
The soul of man will find its greater purity –
    By ending pain and earning heaven's destiny.

DECEMBER 12TH
Happier days

THE FUTURE

A brighter future follows when the conscience stirs. Happier days come with awareness of a need that grows quickly into action, for this is an open ended love that leads and guides towards true spirituality, giving hope where once such upliftment could not live.

UNSEEN HELPING HANDS

When a troubled soul is sad at heart,
And all the world seems wrong,
There's strength to borrow from another source
Complete with angelic song.

For those we've loved throughout the years
But are now beyond our sight,
Are with us, helping day by day,
Aware of our every plight.

We only need to link our minds
To know they're ever near,
To help us gain control of life
And overcome all fear.

For loneliness need never be
A part of earthly life,
When we acknowledge loved ones near,
And greet them with delight.

★ ★ ★

DECEMBER 14TH
Mountains of life

SILENCE IS GOLDEN No. 12

People often create the need of silence. Unkind or thoughtless words that hurt another, would be best left unsaid. Sometimes people use a mistaken motive of truth to hurt another person, when they could so easily remain silent. Angry words that can destroy, spit forth and shatter peace of mind.

But on the other hand, some people remain silent when a few words would help another. All these are negativity – some of the hills and mountains of life that we are born to climb. It is at the top of each hill and mountain that we find the knowledge of spiritual achievement, for here is the golden silence of nature and Spirit, that both rewards and rests the soul.

TRUE GIVING

I met a man the other day,
He hadn't very much to say,
But there he sat on a five-bar gate,
His hands were cold and in such a state,
He'd a happy smile and yet no words,
As he gently tossed his food to the birds.

The snow was thick upon the ground,
It dulled the sense of every sound.
The bun he gave was yesterday's,
It was all he had as a song of praise.
"Well," said he, "It's like this you see,
They're even hungrier than me."

If only those who have a lot,
Would share just like the Master taught,
To lighten someone else's load,
Like this old gentleman of the road,
We then might know true giving's worth,
And find we have a heaven on earth.

SUNRISE

Everyday is blessed with sunrise, giving to our world an essential part of life on earth. We cannot always see the rising sun, for clouds can sometimes block the view. In our personal lives too, cloudy dark thoughts and situations block happiness and progress from our daily living. By remembering that the sun and its life giving warmth will be behind dark moving clouds, we can brighten our own darkest hours, for all life on earth conforms to certain basic patterns, only time and chemical construction make things and situations look different to the human eye. Morning always follows night, springtime's bright greenery and flowers always follow winter's cold. Dark clouds always give way to sunshine in the end, and sunrise is the proof and reminder of this fact of life for all of us – all will be well.

THE BLIND EYE

I wonder why nice people
  Do such peculiar things,
Like scream at mice and trouble,
  And swipe tiny things with wings?

I wonder why kind people
  Kill a friend to eat for lunch?
That baa lamb wouldn't hurt them,
  Lambs are such a cuddly bunch.

I wonder why good people
  Slip from a state of grace,
And start an awful argument
  With anger on their face?

I wonder why brave people
  Will turn their glance away
And *hope* someone in trouble
  Can survive another day?

I wonder why some honest folk
  Can tell such whopping lies,
Or find a way of cheating,
  Ignoring other people's sighs?

It does seem so peculiar
  That folks who think they care,
Can't always see their shortfall
  In the way they choose to share.

For when we think we see ourselves,
  No matter what we do,
We seem to have a blind eye
  That stops us seeing true.

DECEMBER 18TH
A matter of opinion

CRITICISM can be helpful or destructive, but if criticism is of a trivial nature, then there can be little wrong with the subject being criticized!

RHYTHM

The rhythmic movement that we call dancing must be familiar to us all in some way or other, for many it is an absorbing pastime, yet few realise the many implications and great variety of uses and messages of the rhythms of dance.

Rhythm is important to all life on earth. Plants live, fade or die according to their own cycle within the regular coming and going of seasons. Procreation of earthly life depends on the breeding rhythms of every individual species.

The rhythms of dance can create peace of mind with gently flowing movement, or a jolly laughing atmosphere of rhythmic hopping and jumping. Dancing steps and rhythms can convey almost any state of mind from loving, to assertion of power, and further in that direction – states of hate or war. War dances have always been part of primitive cultures, and a dance of death was also practised long ago, said to lead the dancers to the grave. Rhythmic drumming can induce a hypnotic state of mind, and it is a mute point whether the dance itself led the dancers to physical destruction, or whether the dancers' own beliefs mesmerised them towards that end. This possibility reveals another aspect of rhythmic dance, for while it can create, it can also destroy. Dancing can create adverse conditions, even as discordant music can put life out of rhythm, and people who are out of rhythm with life create discord for themselves and others, and are likely to create clashing sounds of music, and ugly choreography in dances, which can affect anyone performing either of these arts, and even people in the capacity of an audience. It is all too easy for clever dancing to overtake true spiritual rhythm and happy interpretation, an important aspect of life on earth. Music and dancing are so interwoven in earthly life, and can be destructive or conversely uplifting in their effects on human beings.

It is easy to see and hear for ourselves these principles of rhythm. A galloping horse for instance, has a certain rhythm which changes when the animal canters or trots, and if it hurts its leg, its movement will lose the rhythm – it is in pain. Different kinds of birds have different rhythms for both flight and walking – sparrows hop, wagtails run on alternate feet.

Realising that animals respond to different rhythms of sound, and create them for their own purpose, we begin to understand the importance of rhythm in our own lives. Peace of mind – and perhaps the whole world could depend on it.

DECEMBER 20TH
What a lot of nonsense!

A DOGGIE GIGGLE

I've come along to say hello,
Because I know you can't say no
To a waggy tail and a cold wet nose,
I know you see, that's the way it goes,
I like to have my bit of fun,
When I'm not dozing in the sun,
And so I thought to you I'd come,
And raise a smile as you tickle my tum!

So here I am with a ladybird,
Although I know it's quite absurd,
So keep it dark – sh, not a word,
Only my snoring will be heard!
I like to have a little sleep,
Though wits about me I must keep,
'Cos though a ladybird is sweet,
She might crawl round where I can't reach!

It's different when a dog has spots,
It's classy to have lots of dots,
Dalmatians with *their* spots are tops,
Standing out from other dogs.
But I'm content to be just me,
Nothing much for you to see,
And ladybirds *are* rather twee,
But if I've made you smile – whoopee!

DECEMBER 21ST
Useful time

A NEW DAY

The dawn is breaking
    To a brand new day,
The world is waking
    To find a brand new way.

But only we who waken
    With earthly time to fill,
Can use the time with wisdom,
    God's purpose to fulfil.

207

CHRISTMAS IS FOR REMEMBERING

Christmas is for remembering
The good things of the past,
The message ringing loud and clear
Towards world peace at last.

Old friends draw near at Christmas time,
To link the days gone by,
Renewing happy memories
That never fade or die.

The New Year is for working
For a springtime bright and new,
Its hopes of health and happiness,
And joyful friendships too.

But Christmas is quite special,
As the memories come to mind,
To light the way of future days
At this happy memory time.

★ ★ ★

A DIFFERENT VIEW

Some see beauty through the eyes of the soul, whilst others only see it through a glass darkly.

★ ★ ★

OLD FRIENDS

The memories fly fast and sweet,
Past accomplishments to keep
Like shining stars and peaceful sleep,
When heaven smiles as old friends meet.

DECEMBER 25TH
A special day

CHRISTMAS DAY

The true value and significance of this day to mankind, lies in the enormous amount of love, kindness and goodwill that is generated world-wide. The actual reason for the celebration, records the birth of a teacher who was to influence the world on an unprecedented scale. His philosophy cannot be faulted, his example should be emulated by everyone. The actual date of his entrance into this world is not known, it has been borrowed from an earlier belief, but this is of little consequence to us now, the fact remains that on Christmas Day we have a pinnacle of loving thought and caring that has built up over weeks of preparation and will continue over several weeks that follow. Ideally it should last the whole year through, but the human being is frail in conscience and spirituality, and too much of that Christmas love and goodwill fades with the passing days.

Nevertheless, in spite of all the commercialism surrounding our modern Christmases, and the greedy consumption of food and drink, the killing and consumption of cruelly reared meat, which would have appalled the man whose birth it all celebrates – this day still generates a kindly tolerance, forgiveness and generosity of both love and material gifts that is not found at any other time of the year.

Other religions have their own special days, and all people must be free to follow their own pathways to God and this one day of the year will not be of importance to them. The extent of kindness and tolerance offered to them certainly will be of importance to all people everywhere, whatever their beliefs about God may be. This is the true value of Christmas Day, and those who celebrate it as a birthday must be its watchdog through the whole year, by following the example of love, tolerance and compassion of the man whose special day this has come to be.

★ ★ ★

DECEMBER 26TH
Honouring sacrifice

BOXING DAY REFLECTIONS

May the kindliness of Christmas Day
Travel with us through the year,
May Boxing Day show us the way
To give, both far and near.

For many have given their lives in pain,
The conscience of the world to move,
And their sacrifice is not in vain,
If we honour those gifts with love.

209

YOUNG AT HEART

If people could be children
    Just one day of the year,
They'd recreate the memories
    That Kiddie Winks hold dear.

Then we could know the magic
    That comes with being young,
The sheer simplicity of life,
    And the art of having fun.

We could put on silly hats,
    Or pretend we are a bird,
Flap our arms and legs about
    Without feeling quite absurd.

As children we could play strange games,
    We could sing and laugh and shout,
Play a joke on Auntie Flo
    And learn what life's about!

We ought to try and learn this trick
    Of thinking young at heart,
And for a day be childlike
    And really act the part.

Then we could play about in mud
    Just like the gardeners do,
Or make a really awful mess
    Of something that's brand new!

Such a day would be relaxing
    For our stuffy older minds,
And we could have such fun of course
    With games of many kinds.

But when we come to think of it,
    Already they're around,
People acting young at heart –
    And they're happy, I'll be bound!

DECEMBER 28TH
Optimism

STORMY WEATHER

Winter brings us the rough cold weather of gales and storms that cause so much damage and chaos in our own orderly gardens. The storms of life do not confine themselves to seasons, but can produce their own particular chaos at any time between our birth and earthly death. At such times it is wise to remember that summer has its place in the organised world of seasons along with the fresh start of every springtime.

Thus the stormy side of our own lives has its spring and summertime, when we have the opportunity to repair the storm cloud damage and look towards the future with optimism and courage in the sunshine moments of our lives. The next winter might not be so bad.

DECEMBER 29TH
The flowering year

JUST ANOTHER YEAR

Roses wave goodbye to spring,
  And welcome every flower fair,
Blending into summer's fling
  Of scent and colour we can share.

But summer blaze of flowers must fade,
  Surrendering to the darker days,
Seeds on Mother Earth are laid
  To sleep in quiet gentle ways.

Autumn gold must gild the trees,
  Blending with signs of Michaelmas
Towards the winter's frosted leaves,
  And tired strands of browning grass.

And yet beyond the cold wet days,
  We know that spring will come again,
Heralding a warmer phase,
  With summer sun and leafy lane.

The flowers will bloom in every hue,
  Riots of colour shining bright,
Planting memories wild and true,
  Ere another year fades from our sight.

211

DECEMBER 30TH
Treasures beyond price

YESTERDAY'S TREASURES

The year is ending very soon, just one more day to do the things we'd planned for it – last New Year's resolutions perhaps! Soon we can make a new start. The human mind enjoys new opportunities and the excuse to draw a veil over unpleasant or undesirable experiences. Each new year gives our minds a chance to draw that veil over any moments of discontent and look forward with renewed hope to the future.

Yet hope is not a magic potion for a happy future, but it does give us the strength and upliftment to work for our dreams of next year in a positive way, the chance to help others, and in doing so make our own lives more worthwhile. This is the real magic of the journey into the new year, and fortunately for us all, we can take with us all the best memories and lessons of the old year that will so soon be gone – they are treasures beyond price.

DECEMBER 31ST
Welcome tomorrow

A GLANCE BACK – A LOOK FORWARD

And so the year has run its course,
    That which was future, now is past,
Precious moments are won or lost
    It is unwise to count the cost.

Hopes that rose with daytime dreams
    Came to nought with devious schemes,
While unsought blessings came it seems
    As fairy gifts on bright moonbeams!

Human plans can go awry
    No matter how we work and try,
Useless then to sit and sigh,
    Shake a fist, or start to cry.

Better by far to accept the plans,
    Of a higher mind that understands
The needs of all the earth's demands,
    Instead of the wants of human minds.

Today will fade with the passing year,
    We'll remember the smiles and perhaps a tear,
And greet with hope and without a fear
    Tomorrow's challenge of a brand New Year.

POSTSCRIPT

LESSONS IN LOYALTY?

An alternative idea

POSTSCRIPT THOUGHTS

Some extra thoughts are offered here for those who have enjoyed the different daily menu. If on the other hand the reader sometimes experienced mental indigestion with the dish of the day, some of the pieces in this postscript might provide an alternative thought – or even a cure for confusion, doubt, or a pain in the emotions of a soul.

Selecting ideas

SOME SECOND THOUGHTS

Many are the thoughts that wander
   Into our daily lives,
Some will die and some will flounder
   But the best ones will survive.

Some thoughts are worth preserving
   To flower another day,
Whilst some are less deserving
   And will quietly fade away.

But some days need some different thoughts,
   Or an extra one or two,
The mind then turns to the postscript sorts
   That somehow filter through.

For sometimes second thoughts are best,
   Yet *could* be a false trail,
Our own free will must do the rest
   As each new day set sail.

And so through all the course of time
   We see the truth of thinking,
We can be guided by another's rhyme
   But must do our own deciding.

215

REFLECTIONS OLD AND NEW

Another year has slipped from sight,
Some memories tease with sheer delight,
While others haunt the future night,
And some will put our fears to flight.

Every year has something new
To guide the many, and puzzle a few,
To show us what it's best to do
And help us sort the false from true.

We saw a new year drifting in,
Some tasks to do, a challenge to win,
And rectify what might have been,
Or teach an erring world to sing.

A team effort

LESSONS IN LOYALTY?

The switchboard operator answered the call from a lady who had been walking her dog by the lake. An ambulance was sent to rescue the swan that had become tangled in a discarded fishing line. Capture was not easy, the entanglement was recent and the swan was still very strong.

The Veterinary surgeon removed the hook from the swan's throat and disentangled its legs, all should be well. But it wasn't, the swan showed no inclination to recover. Meanwhile the lady had walked by the lake again and discovered another swan – very sick and weak.

Collection was easy, but the Vet could find nothing wrong with the bird except its weakness, and it was put with the victim of the fishing line, and that was when the miracle occurred. Swans mate for life, and these two had been pining for each other – and would have died apart. But this story had a happy ending, both birds were returned to their lake, thanks to an observant and caring lady, a Vet and staff of an animal hospital where swans couldn't pay for their treatment, and the loyalty and devotion of two wild birds. There are surely some spiritual lessons here for the world in general, and the uncaring in particular.

Smiling rescues

THE LOT OF THE LOCAL HANDYMAN

This man is quite exceptional,
  A champion of his breed,
Many worlds would fall apart
  Without his skills and deeds.

Some people call him builder,
  Electrician – or just Mate,
Other folk have different names
  If he should turn up late!

He'll quickly come to rescue
  A badly leaking roof,
Or take your word of a 'funny noise',
  Without the slightest proof.

For dripping taps and squeaky doors,
  He's the chap to call,
He won't complain, it's all the same,
  For he can cure them all.

There's yet another side to him –
  His patience and concern,
His listening ear to troubles borne
  And the fear that they'll return.

"There's water dripping through my ceiling,"
  Or "The chimney's blocked somewhere,"
It's only nesting Jackdaws, but
  He'll soon get them out of there!

It's one big rush of rescue work,
  Every single working day,
Unless it's washing down a wall,
  Or dumping heaps of clay.

A garden fence has fallen down,
  Mrs Smith can't shut her door,
It's only her new carpet
  That's thicker than the one before!

A window needs replacing,
  And the sill is rotting too,
There's paper peeling from a wall,
  And there's flooding in a loo.

Our man can cure all these and more,
  If only he had more time,
He's not a handyman at all –
  He's a miracle of his kind!

217

The secret cure

THE HEALING POWER OF TIME

The dreams of night forestall the dawning day,
The morning light propels the bird-song lay,
The sun of noontime warms an aching heart,
Till peace of a new moon brings it sleep at last.
The tides of time reveal the healing power of love,
To gently bring God's healing from above.
Each new passing day soothes troubled souls,
As secretly the healing time unfolds.

Guiding tasks

THE BIT BETWEEN

Between each earthly birth and death
    There are some special things to do,
And we must deal with all the tasks
    That come into our view.

Some will be on a wild track,
    That tests our strength of purpose,
While other pathways will be smooth,
    Or teach us to be cautious.

And we must let our conscience speak,
    To sort the true tasks from the false,
And if we listen carefully,
    It will guide us through the course.

Many are the tasks we'll find
    To create a worthy soul,
Between our earthly birth and death
    We build our heavenly goal.

Gracious giving and receiving

A LADY OF COURAGE

Her early life was a reasonable mix of fun and frowns, she was blessed with nice looks, a certain business acumen and a wonderful husband. Almost anyone could smile under such circumstances. But when her much loved partner left earthly life at a seemingly too early age, disaster had struck this smiling lady of the north of England. They had survived many normal ups and downs, and an aeroplane crash together, could she survive this physical parting? Yes she could, by helping others in her daily round, the elderly, the troubled and a well known charity shop – the Samaritans, she was able to rise above disaster with a smile to help all and sundry. Along her pathway of life she had shared love with a dog and many other friends, but was no paragon of saintly temper, just an ordinary soul like the rest of us that choose to label ourselves normal.

Then disaster struck again in the form of a stroke, and the battle for smiles was on once again. The help she had once given so freely, was now returned in good measure, but our lady of courage had a new lesson to learn, the art of accepting. With the aid of one good arm, a walking stick, doctors, nurses, a lot of determination and kind friends, this lady learnt not only to accept where once she gave, but to smile once again for others. Her gift now is so different to her offerings of earlier years, but the message she tells is one of encouragement to any soul who may be struggling through a sea of troubles, and by demonstrating courage, shows how they can be opposed and ended. And if her smile fades at times behind her own closed door who could blame her, for no one would be there to see.

Every worthwhile lesson of life can be taught or learnt in the university of daily living. The wiser souls can recognise the opportunity of giving and receiving, accepting circumstances or fighting back according to the master plan. Our lady of courage continues to help others by pointing the way with a smile.

★ ★ ★

Canine caring

A PET DOG

Guardian, friend, throughout its life,
Offering sympathy in strife.
An outstretched paw upon the knee,
Its eyes can show what we need to see.
The bouncing joy it loves to share,
The greeting wag that says "I care",
Such loyalty is hard to find,
Except in the love of a pet dog's mind.

The beacon

THE BRIGHT STAR of compassion beckons the world towards tolerance and peace.

With tongue in cheek

A GARDENER'S PRAYER

If there's any gardening angels
    Looking for a job down here,
Please flap your wings in this direction,
    My garden's in a mess I fear.

For things are getting out of hand,
    I'm over-run with slugs,
Greenfly on my roses dwell,
    And some other naughty bugs.

Moles are rising on the grass,
    The mice all eat my peas,
And though the birds sound very nice,
    They're eating all my seeds.

Outright war is not my game,
    And killing doesn't fit
Into my little plan of life,
    But they try my patience just a bit.

So I'd be very grateful
    If you could intervene,
And teach them better manners,
    Like the ladybirds I've seen.

But if you find their ears are deaf
    To the wisdom you have given,
Perhaps you'd bring a bus along,
    And drive them all to heaven!

★ ★ ★

An old fashioned hat

DIPLOMACY has two hats, a dark one to wear with the intent to deceive, evade or get the best possible advantage by devious means, the other is a much nicer model and can be worn by anyone of good intent – it is called kindness.

Just testing

AN EVER PRESENT HELP

When trouble lends its part to life
    With uncertain thoughts and fears,
The strength of God will help you still
    That has guarded you through the years.

The tests of time have proved your worth
    And the power that God is lending,
You know His love will support you still,
    Because it is never ending.

The plans of life are a mystery –
    Things we are asked to resolve,
When we do our best, God does the rest
    As the Spirit of light evolves.

The light it gives will point the way,
    Lest we stumble along our road,
There's nothing to fear, help always is near,
    God arranges to lighten our load.

When we listen and watch for the signals,
    And follow the guidance we're given,
We can overcome all of our troubles,
    With patience and the power of heaven.

Let courage and faith be the watchwords,
    For God never fails when we try,
He knows what is best for our progress,
    And helps us to hold our heads high.

So never be fearful of trouble,
    It is simply a test that is new,
It's always a task we can manage
    With friends and a faith that is true.

Two different views

IN THE EYE OF THE BEHOLDER

Not all eyes see beauty in the same way, for some see beauty through the soul, whilst others see it through a glass darkly, and so perceive it only dimly.

GUIDING MEMORIES

Memory is the corner stone
  That supports our present day.
Our memories are for ever prone
  To present a fine array,
And every memory flower that's grown,
  Has so very much to say
Towards the tasks that are unknown,
  As they guide us on our way.

Unique versatility?

HANDY THINGS TO HAVE

Hands! you know – those versatile things on the ends of our arms! How we misuse them, expecting them to accomplish every daily chore efficiently, and yet be ready to deal with some extra unfamiliar task that may be beyond their physical strength.

We use our hands in so many different ways for so many different reasons, perhaps to hit out when we are angry or gently stroke with a loving touch for a sick child, an animal or loving partner. We carry the baby or our best china with hands that have been primed to be careful. We push lawn mowers, prams and pens and pull on ropes and garden weeds, without a thought for the hands that must interpret these instructions. Hands can be used in cruelty or mercy and may be told to kill, shake a hand in greeting or prune a rose, we never expect them to refuse, until illness or physical damage prevents them getting our message.

If a hand doesn't work properly it confuses our own minds, or conversely – if a mind is not functioning normally our hands become confused. Until then we take our hands for granted, failing to realise they can accomplish so much between good and evil according to our mental inclination at any given time.

We find similar masterpieces of physical construction when we study the bone structure of an animal's paw or the wing of a bird or bat, and can only marvel at the design and power of such tiny bones, muscle and tendon, and the multiple uses of nails and claws.

The miracle of our hands defies our poor imagination, but one thing we know for certain, we put them together when we pray.

Two sides

WISDOM OF THE SOUL

How easy it can be, to be cynical and find material or physical explanations for something which on deeper exploration might have a more Spiritual explanation – a kinder, happier look at life.

Science in all its forms has given the world many blessings and it could even be that some scientists have been guided by an unseen power towards those positive advantages for life on earth. Yet at times, a negative scientific mind will launch upon mankind terrible destruction or pain for body, mind or soul.

Through lack of knowledge many innocent people suffer from these negative discoveries and onslaughts, whilst others of more greedy nature seek personal gain of material things by their negative acceptance.

Experiments and discoveries need to pass the kindness test so that their true value can be ascertained, and this is a test of Spiritual criteria that Science as such has yet to fathom. Wiser minds must meanwhile look for guidance of a more spiritual nature – the universal wisdom of the soul that knows no greed or self aggrandisement, but seeks to guide the world to an everlasting peace, through the lessons of respect for all life upon the earth.

Hills and valleys

THE MAGIC OF DEVON

The hills and vales of Devon's terrain,
Its clotted cream and cider fame,
The rising woodlands, curling lanes,
Moorland ponies with flying manes,
Morning sunrise gleaming gold,
Rising over hills so old
That every undulating line
Creates its own poetic sign,
Square church towers with pealing bells,
Tumbling streams wind through the dells,
Playful otters roll in fun
Or doze in warming mid-day sun,
High primrose banks of wild flowers,
The charm of Devon's magic hours.

PUSS PETS

Cats can be such purrfect pets,
    Yet such independent souls,
They train us to their feline needs
    And their natural ebbs and flows.

We can provide a special bed
    All cosy soft and warm,
But Puss may choose our eiderdown
    With never a fear or qualm.

We buy all kinds of pussy food,
    The tins could fill our house,
But Puss can have a different plan –
    She'd rather catch a mouse!

Cat flaps make an ideal door
    To come and go without a care,
Yet still she'll sit on the window sill
    Demanding entrance there!

But if we should go out awhile
    And leave our friend alone,
She'll softly brush around our legs
    To welcome us back home.

And if we're feeling lonely
    Or something has gone wrong,
Puss will always comfort us
    As she purrs her friendship song.

Our felines offer mystery
    Independence is their style,
And yet they offer us so much
    And make *our* lives worth while.

THEATRICAL GUIDANCE?

"Troubles come not as single spies but in battalions." Thus Shakespeare pinpoints a very prevalent difficulty of modern life. The volume of wisdom in the writings of William Shakespeare lead us to wonder today whether much of his work was actually the influence of an unknown Spirit entity guiding the pen, hand and mind of the Bard.

This particular quotation reminds us that troubles have ever come in two different ways, one being the large devastating event, the other presenting itself as an accumulation of smaller problems, which when put together, resemble the proverbial mountain that we feel we could never climb. They boggle the mind into despair, with a failing courage that would be able to rise to a single large setback in life.

But if we pause to look back at our earlier experiences and circumstances, we will find that we have been given help to overcome such problems. By tackling the difficulties one at a time, and opening our minds to Spirit guidance and accepting their loving help and understanding, we will find that yet again we can deal with that multitude of molehills that together seem such an impossible mountain. If we learn from these experiences as we deal with them, then the effort will not have been wasted. As Shakespeare indicated, "To our own selves be true, we cannot then be false to any man."

Magic moments

I BELONG

I see the magic beauty of the sunshine,
And hear the wistful singing of the wind,
I watch the quiet mystery of moonbeams,
And know the peace of heaven in my mind.

I see the magic beauty of God's flowers,
And hear the joyous singing of the birds,
I watch the splendid mystery of nature,
And know God speaks to me with nature's words.

I see the magic beauty of God's heaven,
And hear the happy sound of angel songs.
As I watch the love of God unfold before me,
I know with peace of mind where I belong.

225

A PHYSICAL MIRACLE

Feet! you know – those things on the end of our legs that we forget all about until we get a corn, an ingrowing toenail or want a pair of new shoes – these miracles of tiny bones and muscles that carry us through life. They work for us equally well on hard pavements, soft sand, along muddy tracks or on rocky mountains. Animals probably give feet even less attention than we do, although they do make sure they are clean – watch any domestic cat and see for yourself.

Even when deformed by some accident of birth or life, our feet still do their best to get us where we want to go, whether it is along a straight smooth path, climbing the rungs of a ladder, or merely pressing on the pedals of our car or bicycle.

Feet, like every other part of the human and animal anatomy, are miracles of design and action that still challenge the human brain, although they have been functioning efficiently ever since they first appeared. We can only bow to the greater knowledge and designer who has given us such gifts.

The individual spirit travels through earthly life and on to an ever greater existence afterwards, and our feet carry us across those earthly miles towards our heavenly goal. What a pity we neglect these miracles of design while we have the chance to care for them!

★ ★ ★

A love of truth

A SONG OF HOPE

If we could learn a love of truth
To guide our way towards the stars,
If we could quell all disbelief,
And tune the erring note that jars,
Then we could fly on wings of song
Towards our hope of heaven's rest,
And greet with joy all those we love,
Who evermore are heaven blest.

If we could learn the truth of love
To guide us to immortal life,
If we would humbly look above
The darker shades of toil and strife,
Then we could see the brighter light
That beckons from beyond the veil,
To enter when the time is right
In God's own time, love will prevail.

226

I SEE A VISION

I see a vision shining bright
   Across the distant hills.
No holy deity in white
   My longing heart fulfils,
Just a golden gleam of light,
   The spreading sunlight thrills
Towards the hope and future sight
   Of peace throughout the world.

I see a vision far away
   Of peace throughout the lands,
Where kindness has its part to play
   To deal with life's demands,
When every human voice can say
   "I love my fellow man."
At every sunset I can pray
   Towards God's greater plan.

I know the vision in my heart
   Will need some time to grow,
With harmony and love to start
   Its journey to and fro
Amongst God's people taking part,
   To give the vision glow.
I see the sunrise shame the dark,
   Salute the peace that all may know.

I see my vision in the sky
   Reflecting all the hope and love,
With true compassion rising high
   That man can seek from heaven above.
I see the wings that onward fly,
   Symbol of the peaceful dove,
A bird of paradise to cry
   For tranquillity around the earth.

GOD GRANT THE WISDOM of thy peace,
   To fall on every ear,
That love and freedom everywhere
   May cast out want and fear.

A CAT AND DOG LIFE

I watched Tishy, a tortoiseshell and white cat grooming the face of Judy the German Shepherd. She rummaged in Judy's ears and made her whiskers twitch. Tishy only gave up on reaching the thick ruff of fur around the Alsatian's neck, before snuggling up with her in sleep.

Many are the times I've reflected on the phenomenon of trust and friendship between two domesticated animals that would be enemies or at least in competition with each other in their wild state. Perhaps they are influenced by a harmonious atmosphere in their domestic home, or maybe two particular animals have learnt to love each other, thus overcoming fear, suspicion and aggression. Whatever the explanation, it is clear that some animals have a special kind of spirituality in their natures that can create peace and a trusting companionship.

Some people also have this spiritual ability, whilst others could – with advantage to themselves and all life around them – learn a valuable lesson from the animals.

Some smiling reflections

THINKING BACK

I often wonder why it was,
   When I was very young,
That all the naughty things of life
   Always seemed such fun.

On the other hand of course,
   Being good was very dull,
And when I tried to be *too* good,
   It could make me feel quite ill.

Grown-ups never could explain
   Why naughty things were bad,
Or what made bad things naughty,
   Which made me feel quite sad.

If grown-ups had no answers
   To such simple little things,
I often wondered how they grew
   Into such clever human beings.

An honest look

THE DISTANT LIGHT

When the people of our world have looked with an honest eye into their own hearts and minds, and have let their consciences deal with what they truly see, they will have struck a mortal blow to greed and cruelty, and this will find the path of kindly tolerance, that will join the highway to Utopia, the light of which is as yet too bright to see.

A choice of words

THE PRINTED WORD

Words are so important,
   They reflect our every mood,
When written they are given life
   To work for ill or good.
The printed words are given power
   To stand the test of time,
And books are homes for printed words,
   Presented line by line –
A choice of motivating thoughts
   To tease the human mind,
And tempt along a doubtful track,
   Or a better pathway find.
For words can lift a searching soul,
   Or bring our thinking low,
The freedom of the writer's hand
   Decrees it must be so.
The comfort of a kindly word
   Can cheer a lonely heart,
Whilst cruel or thoughtless words can hurt
   And tear a soul apart.
There are songs of words for singing
   To trigger our dancing feet,
And find a rhythm of living,
   To make the joy complete.
Words can mould our earthly lives
   By sowing unknown seed,
We can't control the words we hear,
   But we can choose the books we read.

A VISION IN BLUE

The neglected garden seemed to be
The brownest garden you'd ever see,
But with the spring came shoots of green,
Such signs of hope so often seen.

Every day or two I went
To see what nature's plan had sent,
Until there came a mist of blue,
Just to show what God could do.

I stared in wonder at this dream,
Of happiness that might have been
Instead of pain and crying sorrow,
A brilliant blue of joy tomorrow.

As I gazed to humbly ponder,
The mist revealed its silent wonder,
For there it lay in quiet appeal –
A white and lonely baby seal.

Other babies slipped to sight,
Like quiet dreaming in the night,
Fawns and calves and trusting pups,
Human souls and wary cubs.

Every lamb that's known a fold,
Even though it won't grow old,
Came to greet this misty hour,
Along with dolphin, foal and owl.

Every one had picked a flower
To offer me in silent prayer,
A vision in blue, lest we forget,
With a token spray of Forget-me-nots.

The generous pathway

KIND THINKING produces kind action, and is the hallmark of a generous soul.

One day at a time

THE JOURNEY

One day at a time is all we need
    To count our many blessings,
One day at a time to sow the seed
    Of kindly thoughts and actions.

One day at a time to live our lives
    The best way that we can,
To help another in their distress,
    And follow the Master's plan.

One day at a time to the end of the road
    Of earthly travelled miles,
Towards the light of heaven's abode
    To be greeted with much loved smiles.

The journey may be brief or long,
    With compassion the guiding sign,
Footsteps lighten with cheerful song
    As you travel one day at a time.

Future happiness

GOOD WISHES

May your future shine with peace
    Reflecting love and happiness,
May this special day now bring
    Contentment and true joyfulness.
May guiding love be yours this day,
    Your way be filled with graciousness,
May your dreams and hopes come true,
    To fill your life with peacefulness.

231

INDEX

Aiming High	165	Christmas Gifts	197
"All The World's A Stage"	98	Christmas Is For Remembering	208
An Ever Present Help	221	Choice (The)	37
Anger	169	Choir (The)	54
An Organic Gardener's Prayer	94	Circle Of Life (The)	31
Antidote (The)	136	Clarion Call (A)	49
Ants	24	Climb Every Mountain	153
Anyone For Tennis?	103	Coincidence	181
April	61	Cold Words	197
As Autumn Comes	148	Coming Of Spring (The)	45
August	129	Coming Of Winter (The)	178
Autumn Beech	167	Common Sense	75
Autumn Years (The)	161	Compassion	37
		Copycats	36
Balance Of Nature (The)	182	Counting The Years With Giggles	194
Beetles Beware	169	Courage	99
Big Heads?	20	Criticism	205
Bird Of Paradise	155	Cry Of The Animals (The)	202
Birth Of Life	67	Cuckoo	69
Bit Between (The)	218	Cure (The)	32
Blessings (The)	123		
Blest	79	Daisies	80
Blind Eye (The)	205	Daisy Chain (The)	69
Boxing Day Reflections	209	Dark Shadows (The)	172
Boys Of Two	87	Dawn Midst The Hills And Valleys	102
Breath Of Spring (A)	49	Day Begins (The)	122
Bright Star (The)	220	December	197
"But"	46	Delegating The Blame!	156
Butterflies Have Ears	152	Determination	142
Buzz	117	Determination Of Courage (The)	78
		Different View (A)	208
Canine Conversation (A)	183	Diplomacy	220
Canine Devotion	84	Distant Light (The)	229
Card Sharpers Of Life (The)	170	Doggie Giggle (A)	207
Cat And Dog Life (A)	228	Doorway To Heaven	139
Cat Chat	15	Dream (The)	140
Chance To Care (The)	54	Driftwood	98
Chance To Learn (A)	99	Dry Toast	117
Child In Care (A)	186		
Children	70	Egg Flip	191
Christmas Day	209	Essential Ingredient (The)	151

233

Every End – A New Beginning   90

February   29
Field Mice And The Butterfly (The)... ...   143
Fire Game (The)   173
Fleeting Moments   21
Flowers Of Kindness   56
Flower Wept (A)   190
Food Of Love (The)   80
Foreword   7
Forgiving   52
For The Younger Generation   158
For Tomorrow's Children   17
Freedom Of Thought   181
Free Gift In The Shopping Centre (A)   ...   133
Friend (A)   104
Friend Indeed (A)   63
Friends And Relations   115
Friendship   200
Friendship Links   77
Friendship Pie   70
Friendship's Foundation   72
Friendship's Weather Vane   172
Friendship True   153
From Frog   149
From Seed To Flower   16
Frown (A)   67
Fun   167
Fun Kitten   171
Funny Side (The)   61
Fussy Butterfly (The)   76
Future (The)   202

Gardener's Prayer (A)   220
Garden Of Healing (A)   124
Gentleman (The)   199
Gentle Persuasion   18
Gentle Thought (A)   49
Gift Of Seasons (The)   47
Gift Of Sight (The)   168
Gift Of Spring (The)...   67
Gift Of Water (The)   106
Girls Of Two   87
Glance Back – A Look Forward (A)   ...   212
Gnome Nonsense   97
God Grant The Wisdom   227
Golden Gift (A)   182
Good Idea (A)   55
Good Intentions   30
Good News Shoes   30
Good Samaritan (A)   114
Good Wishes   231

Granny's Prayer   113
Guiding Light (The)   41
Guiding Memories   222

Handy Things To Have   222
Happiness   18
Happiness Is For Sharing   129
Hat Cat   66
Have We The Right?   96
Healing Dawn (The)   82
Healing Power Of Time (The)   218
Healing Prayer (A)   141
Healing Words   133
Hearts Of Gold   29
Heavenly Spank? (A)   46
Heaven's Blending   65
Heaven's Dream   154
Heaven's Help   48
Hedgehog (The)   62
Help   184
Helping Friends   189
Helping Hand (A)   140
Hidden Memory? (A)   134
Hide And Seek   15
Hindsight   66
Home Of Happiness (The)   114
Hope   107
How Can This Be?   121
Humane Beings   168

I Belong   225
If Only   118
If They Could Talk   112
Illogical Eating   48
Inexpensive Answer (An)   174
In Loving Memory   185
In Our Own Time   185
Inspiration   51
In Eye Of The Beholder   221
Introduction   9
I See A Vision   227
It Could Mean So Much   105

Journey (The)   231
Journey To Peace Of Mind (The)   53
July   111
June   93
Just Another Year   211
Just One Kind Word   63

Karma?   93
Keys Of Heaven (The)   188

Kind Hearts	19	
Kindly Humour	152	
Kindness	130	
Kind Thinking	231	
Kind Thought (A)	36	

Lady (The) 65
Ladybirds 130
Lady Of Courage (A) 219
Laughter 21
Lawn Daisies 135
Learning 16
Lessons In Loyalty? 216
Lest We Don't Try 171
Let Us Remember 187
Life Continuous 58
Life In Harmony 22
Light Of Spirit (The) 31
Lost Ball 177
Lot Of The Local Handyman (The) 217
Love In The Mist 34
Love Shines 93
Loving World (A) 16
Loyalty 165

Magic Blackbird (The) 78
Magic Of Devon (The) 223
Magic Of Music (The) 189
Major Error (The) 71
March 45
March Of Time (The) 58
Mastermind (The) 160
May 75
Measure Of Grief (The) 33
Measure Of Thought (The) 187
Memories And Future Pathways 14
Memory's Gift Box 136
Merry Gold 151
Messages From The Flowers 116
Minor Unexpected Happening (The) ... 54
Miracle Of The Bees (The) 125
Miracles 131
Morning Artistry 131
Morning Blessings 25
Mote Of Note (A) 120
Mother's Pride 157
Motorist's Dream (A) 79
Mouse Fun 198
Mystery (A) 40
Mystery Of Friendship (The) 86
Mystery Of Loyalty (The) 159

Nature's Evensong 115
Nature's Healing Peace 81
Negative Enemy (The) 192
New Day (A) 207
New Year's Day 13
Night And Day Reflections 193
Night-time 105
Nobility 68
November 181

October 165
Old Friends 208
Opportunity 88
Optimism 77
Orchid And The Daisy (The) 170
Other Points Of View 85
Our Achievements 39
Our Countryside 151
Our Friends The Trees 84
Our Heritage 35
Our Instinct 132
Our Knotted Ideas 150
Our Noble Heritage – The Horse 174
Our Task 184
Ow!! 21

Pain 124
Path Of Kindly Friendship (The) 34
Patience 66
Pause To Learn (A) 111
Pause For Thought (A) 95
Pavement Artist 89
Peace In Our Time? 183
People Power 19
Perchance To Care 23
Perfect Gift (The) 33
Perfection 190
Perseverance 191
Personal Responsibility 149
Pet Dog (A) 219
Physical Miracle (A) 226
Place For Everything (A) 104
Place In The Wild (A) 119
Plea (The) 39
Poetry Of Life 18
Ponderings Of A Garden Bird 51
Possible Heaven? (A) 175
Postscript Thoughts 215
Prayer For Kindness (A) 83
Prayer From An Old Armchair (A) 41
Primroses 50

235

Printed Word (The)	229
Progress?	72
Protection	48
Puppy Love	88
Puss Pets	224
Question (The)	116
Reaching For The Stars	137
Reading The Signs	156
Reason For Suffering (A)	119
Reflections Old And New	216
Religion	141
Rhythm	206
Rhythms Of Life (The)	129
Right Time (The)	39
Right Words (The)	183
Road To Heaven (A)	166
Roots	161
Rugged Coastline (A)	198
Sacrifice	100
Safe Journeys	134
Saving Time	94
Seagulls	123
Seas Of Life (The)	171
Secret Garden (The)	50
Seeds Of Life	14
Seeing Eye (The)	23
Seeing Is Believing	161
Self Deception	56
Sense Of Humour (A)	85
September	147
September Star	150
Service	148
Sharing Loving Thoughts	188
Silence Is Golden No. 1	19
Silence Is Golden No. 2	35
Silence Is Golden No. 3	52
Silence Is Golden No. 4	66
Silence Is Golden No. 5	81
Silence Is Golden No. 6	101
Silence Is Golden No. 7	120
Silence Is Golden No. 8	137
Silence Is Golden No. 9	155
Silence Is Golden No.10	172
Silence Is Golden No.11	187
Silence Is Golden No.12	203
Smile (A)	31
Smile Time	20
Snowdrops Of Life (The)	22
Some People Are Thinkers	89

Some Second Thoughts	215
Some Thoughts About Prayer	72
Song Of Hope (A)	226
Sons Of The Soil	64
Spare Time	178
Special Friends	177
Special Kind Of Love (A)	132
Springtime Sharing	63
Squirrel Sense	57
Stormy Weather	211
Story Of Friendship (A)	38
Summer Bouquet	96
Summer Is On Its Way	76
Sunrise	204
Superiority	193
Theatrical Guidance?	225
There Is A Reason	138
Thinking Back	228
Thought For The Future (A)	120
Thoughtlessness	117
Thoughts Of Flora Exotica (The)	121
Timeless Memories	176
Tit For Tat	35
Tolerance	23
Too Much And Too Little	68
Tortoise Talk	40
Towards A Better World	137
Towards The End Of Shame	17
Travelled Road (The)	154
Travelling	157
True Friends	22
True Giving	204
True Love	103
Truth	61
Truth Of The Matter (The)	113
Try, Try, Try Again	102
Turkey Talk	200
Twenty-four Hours	13
Two Little Ladybirds	106
Two Wonderful People	5
Under The Carpet	169
Unheard Voices (The)	71
Unseen Helping Hands	203
Values	32
Viewpoint	185
Vision In Blue (A)	230
Visitor (The)	125
Voice Of Experience (The)	160
Voice Of The Children (The)	55

236

Waiting In The Wings 142
Warm Welcome 107
Warts And All 138
Weather-wise 57
'Weeds' 52
Weight Watcher's Lament (A) 201
Welcome 125
West Coast 135
West Winds 53
When All Else Fails 173
Whoops! 139
Who's Too Busy? 70
Wild Rose (The) 101
Wild Spring Flowers 64
Wild Summer Flowers 90
Willing Pupil (The) 77
Winds Of Change (The) 191
Winter Jasmine 200
Wisdom Of The Soul 223
Wise Soul (A) 24
Woolly Lamb (A) 82
Words 147
World Of Friendship (The) 97
Worry Factor (The) 122
Worrying Silence (The) 175

Yesterday's Treasures 212
Young At Heart 210
Young In Years (The) 33
Young Ponderings 100
Youth Of The Years 176

5017
7. 3. 04
22.4.4.
10·11·08
10 - 8. 11